Peter's heart ⸻ ⸻ drifted up to where he stood on the ledge. Quietly he moved forward, reached the edge of the rock and looked down. They were there, just below him, the two outlaws and the girl.

"Nothin' doing, you yellow cur," the first one said. "I'll not have the girl hurt, I tell you. They get us or they don't get us. We'll play for the breaks, but whether we get 'em or don't—you'll—not—touch—a—hair—of—her—head. Get that straight."

"All right. All right. But I'm tellin' you, Tim, how it'll be. She snitches an'—" He lifted the palms of his hands in reluctant surrender, half-turned away, and at the same instant his right hand dropped as though by chance to his coat pocket.

Suddenly he whirled, automatic in hand, his face distorted by passion and hatred.

A shot rang out . . .

☆

"One of the most outstanding writers of Western lore."

—*Wilmington Star*

Also by William MacLeod Raine

WEST OF THE LAW
THE FIGHTING EDGE
JUSTICE COMES TO TOMAHAWK
THE BLACK TOLTS
RUN OF THE BRUSH
GUNSIGHT PASS
MAN-SIZE*

Published by
POPULAR LIBRARY

forthcoming

WILLIAM MacLEOD
RAINE

GUNSMOKE
TRAIL

(Original Title: *Moran Beats Back*)

POPULAR LIBRARY

An Imprint of Warner Books, Inc.

A Warner Communications Company

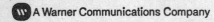

GUNSMOKE TRAIL

CHAPTER I

'Fraid Cat Changes His Name

They say adventures come to the adventurous. But there's nothing to that. They just walk around the corner upon the innocent bystander. And to prove my point I cite the case of 'Fraid Cat Moran.

He was christened Percy, which is, from the American schoolboy's point of view, a crime. To live down such a name one just has to be a ruffian. And young Moran wasn't.

It was a pugnosed girl in red pigtails that called him 'Fraid Cat first. She did it to taunt him to jump from the eaves of the woodshed. Of course he had to jump after that, and he did it so awkwardly that he broke a leg. But the name seemed to fit him because he was timid and shy. So it stuck. That young hooligan Tim Murphy saw to that.

The boy hated it, of course, though no more than he hated his real name Percy. His instinct told him that he ought to fight it down, that he ought summarily to wade into every kid who used it. But what was the use? Tim was cock of the walk, a terror with his fists. He could lick Percy with one hand tied behind him. Young Moran knew it. Why invite destruction? It was characteristic of him that he avoided Tim when he could, and when he could not that he endured stoically what he must.

Percy's people moved from Hilltown, and the pigtailed girl and Tim Murphy were no longer in his life to plague him. He grew up, went to college, and left in his sophomore year to go to France. It was like him that he did not go to an officers' training camp for a commission but joined up as a private without delay.

Probably this was unfortunate, in spite of the fact that he got rid of the Percy by boldly signing as Peter Moran. For in the juggling of men he found himself one day at the front in camp with Tim Murphy.

Since Tim was a born bully, this was nuts and pie for him. He fell upon his former victim with a loud yelp of glee. "Look who's with us! Per-r-r-cy Moran. Old 'Fraid Cat. Well, well, well!"

The same shy timidity was in Peter that had been in Percy. He hated the grime and filth of the trenches. He disliked extremely being wet and cold for many hours at a stretch. When shells whistled over his head, the pit of his stomach sank under him. The zero hour was torture. But he had learned that he could get by if he resisted the temptation to tell anybody how wretched he was.

Now he looked over from the cot where he was lying and said quietly, "My name is Peter Moran."

"The hell it is!" retorted Tim. "It's Per-r-r-cy, an' it'll be 'Fraid Cat whenever I want it to be. See?"

Moran saw, and turned a little pale about the gills. "Peter," he reiterated.

"Per-r-r-cy an' 'Fraid Cat," derided the bully.

The fight that followed was a joy to the company. Peter had not wasted his time at college. He had taken boxing lessons, and discovered in himself to his surprise a natural aptitude for it. Athletics and later camp life had developed him from a stringy boy into a close-knit, well muscled man. Tim was bigger and stronger, but he dissipated a good deal. He made the mistake in the first three minutes of the fight of underestimating his opponent, during which time Peter landed some very hard body blows. The bully was game, but he soon discovered he was in for a licking.

A swift slip to the point of the jaw sent Tim crashing through a cot. He stayed there.

Moran, breathing hard, looked round at the others present. "Is there anybody else here who has personal opinions about my name?"

Apparently nobody had.

Peter continued to detest the mud and shiver at the horrible cold and shrink from the sound of the shells. He was, he knew perfectly well, no hero. Yet, by some queer freak of luck, he won a citation for bravery, and the occasion of it was one day when he dragged Tim Murphy back to cover under a heavy fire when the latter had been wounded going over the top. It chanced that somebody with influence was right there on the spot and saw Peter do it. Hence the citation.

Now Peter never knew why he did it. The fact did not work any miracle in him. Secretly he still funked danger and discomfort. If anybody referred to what he had done, he was acutely embarrassed and felt that he was traveling

8

under false colours. Since they thought he was game they would expect him to play up to his reputation, whereas all he wanted to do was to get by as well as he could unobserved. His medal made him uncomfortable and he buried it deep in the bottom of his kit bag.

All of this by way of preamble, since this is not a war story, to back my claim that if adventures really came to the adventurous, Peter Moran would never have been flung into such a series of melodramatic ones as was forced upon him by that blind goddess Luck.

CHAPTER II

Peter Renews an Acquaintance

The war was an old story, and had been for some years past.

Peter had had more than his share of hard luck. The death of his father at a time when his investments were in a particularly unfortunate condition had made it necessary for Peter to look after his mother and sister. This had kept him very poor. A year ago his sister had married, and this had been followed by the death of his mother.

Tonight Peter walked the streets of Hilltown meditating on the fickleness of fortune. Three months before he had held a good berth with promotion in the offing. Now he was on his uppers with no job in sight. An irritated appendix had done this for him. It had put him in the hospital for two months. At the end of which time he found himself on the streets of Chicago with very little cash in hand and physically unfit to do any but the lightest kind of physical labour. Unfortunately this put him, in the minds of those to whom he applied for work, in the category of the genius tramp. It was the old story a hobo always pulled.

He had bought a ticket for Hilltown because he thought of it as a rather small place where some people would remember him. But Hilltown had grown into a city, and it remembered him not at all. He was in a place looking for jobs where jobs were not, at least of a kind that he could fill.

Walking through the new Country Club district of Hilltown in the mellow darkness of an autumn night, Peter did

9

not reflect on the loveliness of the evening, but upon the fact that he had just seventy-six cents in his pocket. When that was gone——

A closed car drew up at the kerb fifty feet in front of him. Peter observed, without paying any attention to it, that two ladies descended from it, the first middle-aged and inclined to embonpoint, the second straight, slender, and evidently young. They were followed by a young man.

A hard, staccato voice brought Peter back to the present. "Don't move, ladies—or you either, you guy. Stay right where you're at. An' hand me over yore bags an' rings an' watches an' cash."

The older lady screamed.

"None of that," the bandit ordered roughly. "Come through—an' quick."

The hold-ups were standing by the car. One was already relieving the young man of his watch and cash. Quite sensibly, the young fellow's arms were reaching skyward.

Peter was again the victim of that instinctive urge which made him do hazardous things he really had no intention of doing. He had not meant to fight Tim Murphy. He had not meant to run back and drag him to the rifle-pit on the occasion that resulted in the citation. He did not want now to do the foolhardy thing he was doing. For, automatically, Peter's muscles were already functioning. He was moving forward, at a run, head and body low as when he was starting to make a tackle in the old football days.

One of the robbers turned and gave a startled oath. He fired wildly, and the bullet whistled harmlessly past Moran's shoulder. Yet another instant, and Peter had clutched the wrists of the arm which held the revolver. He and the hold-up struggled, the one to deflect the weapon from his body, the other to free his arm. Peter, in his efforts, tried to keep the body of his antagonist between him and the second outlaw. It occurred to him that he was a damned fool for interfering and that he would probably get shot for his pains. But he dared not let go now.

Vaguely there came to him alien sights recorded and recalled later—the dilated eyes of the young fellow still standing with his hands in the air, the tense look of the girl, and the hysteria of the woman. Also sounds which were merely a chorus to the main drama—a woman's scream, a man's lifted voice, running footsteps, another oath.

Twice the revolver exploded, luckily flinging its bullets into the air. Peter began to feel faint. This was the first violent exertion he had undergone since leaving the hospital. In a few seconds he would be helpless.

Then, unexpectedly, the hold-up with whom he wrestled dropped the revolver, succeeded in wrenching his arm free, and legged it down the street after his companion, who was already in retreat. Peter leaned against a maple tree in the parking and relaxed weakly. He was irritated at himself because he thought he was going to faint.

But he did not do that. The older woman anticipated him by sinking into his arms, just as a bare-headed, white-haired man ran down the walk. She had fainted.

The older man gave orders. "Carry her in, you two."

His daughter—it developed later that she was his daughter—spoke a little sharply to the other young man. "It's all over, Jack. You can help, can't you?"

Jack hurried forward. His arms, no longer perpendicular, went round the lady's waist. "Take her feet, my good fellow," he told Peter.

They carried the lady into the house. The younger woman led the way, opening doors and sweeping impediments from a lounge in a living-room. She flew to get water and smelling-salts, while her father unloosened the fur scarf of the unconscious woman.

Peter waited, not quite certain whether he 'ought to go yet or stay. The other young man moved toward him just as the young woman returned with restoratives. He was immaculately dressed in summer sports clothes. His flannels, shoes, shirt, the tan of his face—everything was perfect. Into his right-hand trousers pocket his hand slid a little hesitantly. Evidently he was not quite sure of his ground.

"Jack," the young woman said hastily, "get our things out of the car, will you?"

He vanished on his errand. Peter made to follow him and moved towards the door.

The older man did not appear to be looking at him, but he gave a crisp command in the tone of one used to being obeyed. "Wait!" He was about fifty-five or perhaps a little older, well-dressed and well-set-up. There was distinction in the clear-coloured face, with its clear contours crowned by the shock of wavy silvery hair.

Peter waited. He had no business outside which demanded

11

pressing attention. His chief trouble was that he had no business anywhere, unless one could dignify by that term the matter of looking up a very cheap lodging-house for the night. Moreover, Peter was interested to see what this man's reaction to the situation would be. The younger fellow had been on the verge of offering him money when the girl had distracted his attention. He did not expect the silver-headed man to be so crude as that.

After restoratives had been applied the lady on the lounge opened her eyes. "James—Janet!" she said uncertainly. "What is it? I—I——"

"Don't worry, Mother. It's all right," the young woman answered.

"You fainted, my dear," the husband explained. "A little shock, but it's all right now."

She took another whiff of the smelling-salts. "I remember now. Those dreadful men." She shuddered. "Was anybody hurt?"

The daughter spoke. "One of them fired two or three times at this—this gentleman." Her eyes had shifted to Peter. "He didn't hurt you, did he?"

"No," said Peter.

He observed that her eyes were a lovely brown, how very clear the complexion, with what simple elegance the slender figure was gowned. She was perhaps twenty-four or twenty-five, this young woman, and her face interested him very much. One could scarcely call it pretty or beautiful, and yet——

"How did it come about? Tell me what happened," the father said.

It was his daughter that answered. She seemed to have inherited her father's capacity for leadership. The mother was a soft and pliable person, Peter judged. Jack had just returned, but if he had any intention of telling the story the girl forestalled him. She took off her hat as she began to talk, and the magnificence of her red hair took Peter by surprise. Hair like that would make any woman's fortune. He wondered now that he could ever have thought for a moment she was not beautiful.

"We were just getting out of the car when a man pushed a gun at us and told us to give him our rings and our bags. There was another man with him. I think Mother cried out. She was shocked and frightened. We all were."

12

The immaculate Jack murmured what might have been regarded as a protest against being included in this admission.

Janet paid no attention to this, "I started to take off my rings. One of the men took Jack's watch from him. Just then things happened in a rush. This gentleman ran at one of the robbers and fought with him for his gun. It went off two or three times. Then we heard you coming. The robbers ran away—and Mother fainted."

Jack got in his explanation. "The fellow shoved a gun against my stomach. There was nothing to do but stick up my hands."

"Of course," the girl said impatiently. "Nobody blames you." It occurred to her that another man, a stranger and not the man to whom she was engaged to be married, had found something else to do.

"The beggar took my watch," Jack said.

"Did he?" Janet's eyes sparkled. One might almost have thought that she was glad of it.

The older man turned to Peter. "My name is Carey. I don't need to tell you how much we are indebted to you, all of us, for what you did. It was uncommonly plucky and might have cost you your life."

Peter shook hands with visible embarrassment. "Nothing to that. Nothing at all. I just happened to be there, so I thought I'd butt in."

"Well, it's fortunate you did, as it turned out."

"My name is Moran—Peter Moran," the butter-in murmured, understanding that this was expected of him.

Carey completed the introduction. "Mrs. Carey, my wife—and my daughter Janet. Mr. Meredith."

Janet's hand lingered for an instant in Peter's. There had been for a few moments a puzzled expression on her face. She felt sure she had seen him before. But where?

"I think we have met before," she said uncertainly.

In a flash he knew her. She was the red-haired girl of his schooldays, but no longer a tormenting imp in pigtails. Evidently she had gone up in the world as he had gone down.

He grinned. " 'Fraid Cat Moran," he suggested.

"Of course." Her face lit up with recognition. "Percy Moran."

"It's Peter now, not Percy," he corrected.

Her smile was brilliant. "And it's not 'Fraid Cat either."

"I'm not so sure of that, though I don't stand for the name from others."

"I'm sure enough, after tonight. I never saw anything so splendid." Then, with apparent irrelevance, "I was a perverse little devil in those days."

"Yes," he admitted impartially.

"Where have you been? I never hear of you. I've never seen you since. Didn't you move away?"

"Yes. I came back this week."

"I'll want you to tell me all about yourself," she said.

He liked her eagerness, her vivid manner. On the other hand, Mr. Jack Meredith did not. Why did Janet have to give herself just as enthusiastically to this beggar as to her friends —to him, for instance? Of course she had to be courteous after what he had done, though it was a damn fool business, if anybody asked him, Jack Meredith. (By all the chances of the game he should have been potted through the heart.) It was like Janet to overplay her hand that way. She was always falling hard for some impossible duffer nobody else could see. That was what made her so trying. He had a good mind to put his foot down about it.

"It's nice you know each other," Mrs. Carey said equably.

Peter felt it was time to go. He hoped that Mrs. Carey would be none the worse for her fright and made his adieux to the others.

Cary handed him a business card. "Can you call on me tomorrow, Mr. Moran? At ten-thirty, say."

Peter said that he could and beat a retreat.

Under a light at a street corner he took out the card and from it gathered the information that James Carey was president of the First National Bank of Hilltown.

Decidedly the Careys had gone up in the world since she had been at the public school with him when they were kids. Still, he did not need the card to tell him that. The large house and its luxurious appointments, the clothes and manner of the family, had told him so. He wondered, rather irrelevantly, if the solitaire she wore on the engagement ring finger of her left hand had been given to her by that bounder Meredith.

CHAPTER III

Carey Asks Questions

Peter was on hand promptly at ten-thirty. He did not know exactly what Mr. Carey wanted with him, but there was always the chance of a job in the offing. Very likely the banker had a good many irons in the fire. Perhaps he indulged in the luxury of a ranch. He might be receiver for some business or manufacturing plant. No doubt he was interested in the new oil-fields that were booming at Petrolia. Anyhow, Peter did not want to overlook a bet. He would have felt insulted if he had been offered pay for what he had done, but he was not so quixotic as to refuse any work he could handle, anything of a nature for which he could give value received.

The bank had a prosperous metropolitan look. It was built of granite and there was a good deal of marble inside. There were many windows for receiving and paying accounts, savings department, collections, and statements, as well as railed-off spaces for the desks of cashiers, vice-presidents, and trust officers. In the open lobby men and women hurried to and fro or waited in queues at the windows.

Peter had to wait a few minutes in an anteroom. Presently a plump, baldish man with a well-fed look emerged from the inner room with Mr. Carey and they shook hands at the door. The banker called him by the title Senator, and from cartoons and pictures he had seen the young man recognized him as the senior United States Senator of the state. The two men were laughing and chatting in a very friendly fashion. Somehow this gave Peter a feeling that he was small fry and of not much importance.

He followed Carey into the inner office and took the chair offered. There were others waiting in the outer room, yet the banker appeared to be in no hurry. He passed across the desk a box of cigars, but Peter declined to smoke. The older man lit up and leaned back comfortably.

"Pretty hectic doings last night, eh, young man?"

Peter assented.

"I needn't tell you that we're grateful for what you did. I'm frank to say I think you risked your life. Not very wisely, I'm afraid. Still, I should be the last to complain."

"If I had had time to think probably I would have had more sense," Peter replied.

"It worked out very well for all of us." Carey shifted the angle of approach, after puffing for a moment in silence. "I was interested to learn that you are an old school friend of my daughter."

"Afraid that's stretching the facts. We were in the same room. That's about all."

"I talked with her after you left. She seems to have behaved rather badly towards you. From what she says I gather that she was responsible both for the nickname your mates gave you and for a broken leg."

"That's hardly fair. My temperament was responsible for both, I suppose."

"Her conduct was on her conscience after you got hurt, but she did not mention it at home. She says she has often thought of it since."

"She need not worry," smiled Peter. "That leg healed and the nickname is forgotten. So that's that."

Again the banker shifted his conversational approach. "Do you mind, Mr. Moran, if I ask some questions about yourself? I assure you it is not from idle curiosity."

"I'll be glad to tell you anything you'd like to know about myself," the young man assured him. It began to look to him as though he were on the trail of a job.

"Suppose you start then by giving me a sketch of your life since you left here. Unless I'm taking too much for granted. Perhaps you are placed satisfactorily in employment."

"It happens that I'm not. I came to Hilltown looking for work. A place to suit me is difficult to find. I'm just out of a hospital, and I'm not at all strong yet."

"Do you want outdoor or indoor work? What's your profession?"

"I'm like a good million other Americans. I haven't any. I have kept books more or less and been head salesman in a broker's office. Just now, until I get stronger, I'd like some light outdoor work. I'm not particular about the pay so long as it is enough to keep me."

Peter told his story in a dozen sentences. The banker asked questions and jotted down notes. Before Peter had finished,

Carey knew several places where he had been employed, his reasons for quitting each place, the regiment and company in which he had served in France, and the names of several of his superior officers, as well as the hospital from which he had lately been discharged after the operation. Peter admired the thoroughness with which he went after his facts.

"By the way, Janet says your name was Percy. I believe you call yourself Peter now?" The banker's keen eyes plombed into him.

"I couldn't take Percy into the army with me," the young man explained. "I would have had a dog's life. Peter turned out to be so much better to live with that I've kept it since."

Carey did not question this, but Peter had a feeling that the banker was going to look up his record thoroughly before he went too far to retreat.

"I can give you some half-time temporary work in the book-keeping department. Would that suit you for the present? Perhaps later I can find something that may be more to your taste. There is no opening just now in our bond department."

"That would suit me very well. I shouldn't care to stay a book-keeper very long, but for the present it will do nicely."

Peter went to work next day. It was ten days later that the president summoned him to his office.

"I've been looking up your record, Moran," he said without any preliminary talk. "I find it's good. By the way, you didn't tell me that you were decorated for bravery while in the army."

Peter blushed. He was a man of the type who is embarrassed when anything creditable is discovered about him. "That was a fluke," he explained.

"How do you mean a fluke?"

"I happened to see a wounded man and hoisted him on my back. A brigadier-general happened to be there. He wrote some hot air about it to headquarters."

"I see," the banker said dryly. "Well, if you don't mind I'll take the brigadier-general's point of view. I can use you just now in another capacity if you'll let me shift you. We're shipping a lot of money for expenses and pay-rolls to Petrolia these days. That's known, of course. Some very bad characters have gathered both here and at the oil-field. They are attracted by the easy pickings that always go with a sudden gold or oil boom. I want a man on whom I can rely to act as a guard for gold and currency shipments. Do you know how to use a revolver?"

"As it happens, I do. I used to practise with the ex-champion of the country. I suppose I'm rather a good shot—at least he told me so. Of course I did not class with him."

"Good! Can you look after this for me then? I don't want, you understand, to send an arsenal along with these shipments. I'm not really expecting a hold-up, and I don't want to advertise for one. But it occurred to me that if you could be there on the job all the time it would make me feel more comfortable. Have you any objection?"

The young man hesitated. "I'm not the best man you could get by a long shot. The fact is I'm rather a timid person. You can deduce that from the name they gave me at school."

"Yes, well, that's all right," the banker smiled. "I want for the job rather a timid person, of your particular type of timidity. We'll consider it settled if you'll accept."

Peter gave a little shrug of his shoulders. "Oh, all right then."

But after he had left the room he asked himself resentfully. "Now what did I let him wish it on *me* for?"

CHAPTER IV

The Timid Man Functions

It was a sunny afternoon in late January. A glow as warm as Indian summer brooded benignantly over the land. Its languor seeped down even to the bottom of the deep cañons formed by the high office and store buildings lining Seventeenth Street.

There was a steady hum of traffic, pierced occasionally by the honking of a horn, the snorting of an automobile, or the traffic officer's whistle. Trolley cars, trucks, buses, private motors, and pedestrians moved in a shifting kaleidoscope. An artist might have chosen the scene to represent peaceful commerce moving in orderly confusion to its appointed ends.

In front of the First National Bank a closed van came to a halt. From the seat beside the driver a young man swung alertly down. He wore a pinched sombrero, one that had seen the heat of a good many summer suns, and an olive-drab suit with trouser legs encased in puttees. The young man moved to the entrance of the bank and waited there, as a casual loiterer might, while the driver went into the bank.

An indolent indifference was suggested by the manner of this olive-drab youth. He leaned up negligently, as it were, against one of the pillars near the entrance. But if anybody had watched him closely—and it developed later that somebody did so watch him—it might have been observed that his blue eyes were very attentive to what went on around him. His brain registered data that might by some millionth chance later prove valuable. The fingers of his right hand, now buried to the knuckles in the lower pocket of his coat, remained there motionless.

His busy eyes and brain, as he stood there, selected and appraised. They automatically eliminated from consideration three giggling high-school girls eating chocolates, a dozen women on shopping bent, two lawyers with brief cases—in fact, most of the hurrying pedestrians. But they took cognizance of a heavy-set man in a roadster on the opposite side of the street, a man with his back to the bank, hunched low in the seat. Something about the set of that back seemed somehow vaguely familiar to the watching eyes. They noticed, too, a ferret-eyed, putty-faced man who slouched past and later joined the man in the roadster.

These registered impressions would probably be of no importance. If not, they would be sponged from the retina of the memory unconsciously. It was on the long chance that they might that they were temporarily recorded.

Yet, after all, the watchful young man was taken by surprise. A young woman's voice hailed him.

"How do you do, Mr. Moran? Why haven't you been to see us?"

The voice and the hand that was offered belonged to Janet Carey. Young Meredith was with her, immaculate in the latest equipment from head to foot.

"Excuse my left hand," Peter said.

"What's the matter with your right?" she asked. "Have you hurt it?"

"Not exactly, but it's busy just now," he said, returning Meredith's curt nod.

"Busy?" she repeated, looking down at it without understanding.

The driver of the van emerged from the bank, accompanied by two clerks, each of them carrying a heavy bag.

Peter spoke bluntly to Janet Carey and her escort. "Excuse me, please," and his eyes wiped them off the map. His glance went up and down the street, then followed the bags to the van.

One of the clerks got into the van with the bag, locking the door automatically from the inside. The other returned to his duties in the bank. Moran stepped across the sidewalk and took the seat beside the driver. His finger knuckles still protruded from the coat pocket where they had remained ever since his arrival.

The roadster with the two men in it passed the van and swung round a corner out of sight. It was headed toward Eighteenth Street. The van turned at Cheyenne Street and again at Eighteenth, each time to the left.

"Got a cig, Pete?" the driver asked.

"Sure, Bill." Moran's left hand drew from a pocket a package of cigarettes and shook one out. The driver drove with one hand while he took and lit the cigarette.

Scarcely a minute later the van drew up at the express office in the Union Station and backed toward the pavement. In the open space to the right at the passenger entrance a taxi was disgorging occupants and baggage. Other cabs were moving to and from the station, passing under the Welcome Arch as they came and went. A large car with several men in it stood in the parking space opposite the express office. Its engine was running. Not far from it a roadster waited. The engine of this car also sounded.

As Bill swung down from the seat behind the wheel his cigarette was still two-thirds unsmoked. Already Moran was standing beside the wide double door leading into the express office. The door of the van opened and the bank messenger stepped out. He was joined by the driver and by a clerk from the office.

In the mellow afternoon sunshine the scene was peaceful as old age. A stray dog lay on the sidewalk and hunted not too diligently for fleas. A freckled-faced red-cap sauntered past with his hands in his pockets whistling the tune of a song from "No, No, Nanette." Peter had heard it at the local theatre, a few days before, and the drift of it was that the singer wanted to be happy, but he could not be happy "unless you are happy *too*."

Then—a shot rang out—another—and another. From both the roadster and the big car men were shooting. One had a sawed-off shotgun, one a rifle, the others revolvers.

The driver of the van ran round the car to see what was wrong. There was another shot. He stopped, a queer, dazed expression on his face, and sank down against the front wheel of the van. With a yelp of fright the bank clerk dropped his bag and bolted through the express office to the platform beyond and down through the subway to the farthest tracks. The express clerk, the red-cap, and the electrified dog vanished. They had been on the horizon; now they were not.

Nobody was left by the van except the timid man. At the flash of the first shot Peter Moran's hand had leaped from the coat pocket, in the closed fingers the handle of a blue-nosed forty-five. Before the sound of the second shot had died away he was answering the fire of the bandits.

A hot thrust, as from the steel of a plunging rapier, pierced Peter's forearm and numbed it. The guard knew he had been hit and shifted the revolver to his left hand.

From out of the automobiles the outlaws piled. They came toward the van with a rush. Moran fired again—once, twice. The swarm of men were almost upon him when he knew by the harmless click of the hammer that he had spent his last shot.

A rifle barrel descended upon his head. He flung up an arm to break the force of the blow. The earth crashed up to meet the sky and the two went whirling. He staggered back, went down under the impact of another blow from a black-jack, and slid down close to Bill, who still sat propped up by the wheel.

If Peter lost consciousness it was only for a few seconds. When his eyes shook off the haze they looked into the white, ghastly face of the driver Bill. A thin curl of smoke still rose from the cigarette held between the man's lips.

Then Peter remembered what had taken place. His eyes swung round to the cars into which the bandits were piling with their booty. He noticed that one of the men drooped forward, his head hanging over the side of the car. In another moment both automobiles had swept around the curve and were racing up Eighteenth Street.

Peter tried to rise—and fell back again weakly. Funny how the silly old world began to jazz when he moved.

21

"Those guys—they'll make a clean get-away," murmured Peter to the driver.

Bill did not answer. Smoke still curled in a faint spiral from the cigarette. At least half of this was still unsmoked. The driver's head, arm, and body drooped laxly. A bullet had penetrated his heart before he even knew the treasure van had been attacked.

Then Peter collapsed. He sank back against the wheel and slid down. For the time he lost all interest in the subsequent proceedings. He had fainted.

CHAPTER V

Oh, Is He Your Friend?

Jack Meredith looked after the van as it swept around the street corner on its way to the station. He was a neat, good-looking man, and he wore a carefully reared black moustache. A spoiled only son, he still pouted occasionally when annoyed. Just now he was distinctly annoyed. He did not see any reason for putting up with this Peter Moran's rotten manners.

"Impudent beggar," he commented, in resentment of the other's brusque behaviour.

Janet had been thinking something rather like this herself, but she chose to object to the expression of such an opinion by her fiancé.

"Think so?" she asked, in her voice the studied indifference which does not take the trouble to mask opposition.

"Offering his left hand, by Jove. Cheek, I call it."

"You would. I suppose you didn't notice what he was doing with his right hand."

"Oh, whatever he does is right," he said sulkily.

"He had a revolver in it. If you'd use your eyes and your grey matter, Jack."

"I dare say he was some kind of a bally guard. That's no reason for being insulting."

"He was busy. Some men are, you know."

"Why slam me because you're sore at him?" he asked in a huff.

"I'm not sore at him, as you so elegantly express it. The

22

point is that he had been given a job to do. He couldn't stay here and pay compliments to us."

"Walked away from us like the Shah of Persia, and you seem to like the tramp's high-and-mighty airs."

"Please don't speak of my friends that way," she told him, her chin in the air.

"Oh, is he your friend?"

Janet walked into the bank and he followed her. Meredith was annoyed at her and dissatisfied with himself. It seemed to him that ever since this Moran had butted into their lives five or six weeks ago the weather had been squally. Janet and he used to get along fine, but now she was so touchy. The mere mention of Moran's name made for friction, though this might not reach the surface. Jack did not realize the reason, which had to do with both his own and Janet's mental reactions as affected by the hold-up episode participated in by all three of them.

Moran had usurped the star's part, and Jack Meredith wanted to play star himself in his relationships with Janet. Even if he had not been very vain, this would have been natural enough. He was engaged to her, as much in love with her as he could be with anybody except himself, and he had no fancy for yielding the spotlight to another man. The whole thing was absurd of course. He had done only what any man of sense would have done, but this jackass by blundering into the scene had made it look as though he were playing an unworthy part.

Carlton, the cashier of the bank, was an old friend of the Carey family. He rose from his desk to come forward and shake hands with Janet.

"Dad busy?" she asked, after greetings had been exchanged.

"I notice he's usually not too busy to see you," Carlton answered, smiling. It was notorious that the bank president was so partial to his daughter that he did his best to spoil her.

Presently she and Meredith were shown into Carey's office. Janet concluded her business with him.

"Why don't you go out to lunch with us, Dad? We'll let you pay for it," she suggested.

"Too busy. Director's meeting. Run along now and play."

"Play? Hmp! If you were as busy as I am, if you did as much in a day——"

The telephone buzzed. Carey picked up the receiver. Instantly the lines of his face hardened. His solid figure straightened. When he spoke his voice was crisp and incisive.

"Both killed, you say. Have the police been notified?"

The girl was aware of disaster. The atmosphere had instantly become tense—electric. She stood rigid, silent, her eyes on her father, while she waited for him to finish with the telephone before she poured out her anxious questions.

The bank president cut in again. "A clean getaway, you say? With all the money?"

Even as he was hanging up the telephone receiver he was pressing a button, one of a small array of them attached to the side of the desk.

A man appeared. "Tell Mr. Carlton I want to see him. At once, no matter with whom he is engaged." He turned to his daughter. "Is your car here?"

"I came in Jack's." Then, uncontrollably, "What has happened, Dad?"

"A hold-up. The van has been robbed. And two men killed. One of them Moran, I'm afraid."

She did not cry out or make any display of feeling. But it seemed to her for a moment as though her heart had stopped beating. It had come so near to her, this shock out of a clear sky. Not ten minutes ago she had talked with this man. Without conscious thought it came to her how vital he had looked, how the muscles of his legs and shoulders rippled beneath his clothes as he moved, how individual were his manner and appearance. He could not be dead. It was not reasonable.

Her father was telling Carlton about it when she came out of herself. He gave directions.

"I'm going down to the station. Don't spread the news. If it gets out and people pour in to ask questions minimize it. Be careful not to give out to the newspapers the amount of the shipment or any official statement. I'll probably be back soon."

"I'm going with you, Dad," the young woman told him as he started for the door, beckoning to Meredith; and fearing refusal she pushed on with her explanation. "I couldn't sit here and wait. I'm worried and anxious too. You'll let me go, won't you?"

"Come on if you want to," Carey said. "It won't do any harm."

Meredith drove them down to the station. Already a large crowd had gathered and the police in force had established a cordon to keep people back. A captain of police recognized Carey and made a way for his party.

"Have the robbers been caught yet?" asked the banker.

"Not yet, far as I know, sir. We've 'phoned to all the outside stations to keep a lookout, and to every town near the city in case they try to make their getaway in cars. Half a dozen cars filled with armed officers are scouring——"

"What about Peter Moran?" Janet broke in. "Is he—— Did they shoot him?"

The captain shook his head. "Don't know him. They killed the driver and wounded a guard. Here comes the ambulance for him now."

The banker's party had pushed through to the van. A doctor and two or three others were ministering to somebody whose face Janet could not see, while four or five police officers pushed back the press of onlookers.

The doctor shifted his position and Janet looked down into the white face of Peter Moran.

CHAPTER VI

Janet Has Her Way

Peter wondered mildly about this world upon which he opened his eyes when he came back to consciousness. It seemed full of heads rather oddly detached from bodies, big-eyed faces that stared at him from all directions to which his gaze wandered.

His impressions localized. There was first of all an annoying little person taking liberties with his head. At least it was probably his head. Certainly it was a very painful one, whoever it belonged to. Back of him were policemen, several of them, holding back a circle of pressing people. He knew by this time they were people, though they were still mostly eyes.

What was it all about? He tried to rise, but gave that up with a groan.

"Don't move," the annoying little man ordered. He had a black bag and scissors and a roll of gauze.

Peter's roving eyes met those of Bridge, the bank clerk. What had taken place began to come back to him.

"We were held up, weren't we?" he asked.

The clerk nodded. His face was still drained of blood. He had been given the shock of his life: "God, it was awful!" he said.

The treasure guard put a heavy hand to his aching head. His hand felt moist. He looked at it and was surprised to see that his fingers were red. He frowned.

"Don't do that," the doctor told him. "Keep your hands away."

"Did they get the bags?" Peter asked Bridge.

"Yes."

"Where's Bill?"

The bank clerk's lip quivered. Bill, but for the grace of God, might have been Philip Bridge. "He's dead."

"Dead! He can't be. He was smoking here beside me."

There was an undulation in the crowd. It opened, to let through a policeman followed by Carey, Janet, and Meredith.

Carey spoke to the doctor, in a low voice, nodding toward the wounded man. "How is he?"

"Can't tell yet. He has lost a good deal of blood. Here's the ambulance. We'll get him right to a hospital."

"See he gets the best attention and the best surgeons in town. I'll be responsible for the bill."

Looking down on the white face and bloody head of Moran, Janet was the victim of a strange, insurgent emotion. She forgot all about the number of people present and dropped down on a knee beside him.

"Oh, Peter!" she murmured tremulously.

He managed to grin. "Had to jump from the woodshed again," he told her. "Look out. I'm all bluggy."

His voice was rather weak, but his manner reassured her. A man about to die could not talk like that.

"You'll have the best care," she promised him. "Don't try to talk now, please. You must keep your strength."

Her father touched her shoulder. "They're ready for him, dear."

A lane had been made through the crowd. The men with the stretcher put it down beside Peter. They lifted him upon it and carried him to the ambulance.

"Let's go to the hospital, Dad," she urged.

"Not now, dear. We can't do any good there. In fact, we'd be in the way. He'll get the best possible attention. I've talked with the doctor. And I have work to do. You'd better go home. Jack will look after you."

Janet had no intention of going home. As soon as they were in the car she said to Meredith, "Drive to the hospital, Jack."

"What for?" he asked, at once resentful.

"To find out how he is. I want to know."

"If we go we can't find out. The doctors themselves won't know until they've examined him thoroughly, perhaps not until after he's been operated on."

This was probably true, but Janet did not want to be ruled by common sense just now. She was wrought up emotionally and intended to be ruled by her impulses. It seemed to her that if Jack had any consideration for her he would be in a sympathetic mood.

"I'm going to the hospital," she said by way of flat announcement.

"All right," he yielded ungraciously. "I suppose you'll have to have it your way. You always do."

She did not reply to that. As long as he took her where she wished to go she was indifferent to what he thought.

His prediction proved true. They had to stay below in the waiting-room. Nobody paid any attention to them till Janet persuaded a sister to find out how the wounded man was getting along. She returned with the usual ambiguous report that he seemed to be doing well. There could be no more definite information for some hours, she added.

Janet went home reluctantly with her fuming fiancé. He took pains to let her know that he had told her they would waste their time if they went to the hospital. The fact that he was right did not increase her good-will toward him. It occurred to her, as it had done more than once lately, that she was just about fed-up with Jack. They seemed always to be annoying each other, to be taking opposite points of view. She did not understand it, because at first they had seemed very congenial.

Jack Meredith was heir to the fortune of an old wealthy family. He had retired from all business except that of looking after his property, the active work of which was done by an agent. Socially and financially he was a catch, the sort of youth for whom mothers angle as a husband for a daughter. He was not vicious. He was healthy. And he had all the advantages that accrue when one is of the best set and in easy circumstances. Janet had done herself rather well. Moreover, she had fancied herself in love with him in spite of his lordly

27

ways. These amused her, since she was not the victim of them. Certainly it had flattered her vanity that of all the girls in Hilltown he had picked her, whose family only recently had come to be accepted socially. For Janet was entirely human, even though personally democratic.

When they reached her home Jack did not offer to come in, nor did she ask him. Each realized that there was a bit of a strain between them, that they were not in accord just now. Janet was relieved that he did not come in. He was in a sulky humour and she herself in one frankly hostile to his point of view. They would be very likely to annoy each other more. It was even conceivable that they might have a grand flare-up.

Janet did not want to quarrel with him. She quite appreciated the advantages of being engaged to him, and until lately they had been such good friends. He had a gay, engaging way with him when he wanted to please, and it had been fun to play with a man whose time was always at her disposal. No, decidedly she did not want any break with him—especially over nothing more serious than the fact that she wanted to be decent to Peter Moran.

CHAPTER VII

Peter Has a Hunch

The temperature dropped thirty degrees the night after the hold-up of the pay-roll shipment, and it continued to fall most of the next day. The weather in the Rockies is subject to sudden changes. This is merely a slight flaw in the climate, which is freely admitted by the inhabitants to be the best in the world.

Peter was not particularly inconvenienced by this sudden descent of winter, since he spent the next ten days in bed. During that time there was no modification of the severe cold, except slight changes of a few degrees during the hours in the middle of the day.

As soon as Peter was able to stand questioning, Carey and Burlson, the local head of the detective agency which represented the bank and the surety company, came to the hospital and questioned him about the hold-up. He was getting along as well as could be expected. The bullet had passed through the fleshy part of his arm and left a clean wound. The doctors had been disposed to worry more about the blows on the head, but it developed that these had brought about no concussion likely to produce permanent results. So he built up his strength again rapidly and was soon able to undergo an examination.

The Chief of the City Detective Bureau arrived and was shown to Peter's room while the other two men were getting seated.

Burlson did most of the questioning. He carried Peter over the whole episode, starting from the time the van had driven up to the bank and ending when he lost consciousness.

Peter told what he knew. He had nothing to conceal. Unfortunately he could not add much to what the sleuths had already picked up. One detail he supplied. He mentioned that the roadster which had taken part in the attack, in which two men were sitting when the van drove up to the express office, had been waiting in front of the bank when the pay-roll shipment had been brought out to the van. This was important because it showed that the bandits expected it to be sent and had men on the job to ascertain the moment of starting and to carry word to their confederates at the station.

"Would you know any of these men again?" Burlson asked.

"I think I'd know the putty-faced fellow who passed by me and joined the other fellow in the roadster. He looked like a dope fiend."

"Probably is. That's the kind that gets into jobs of this sort nowadays," the city chief commented.

"Describe this putty-faced man as well as you can," Burlson said.

"Well, I can't give a very good description of him. He had heavy eyelids. I noticed that because his eyes didn't look at me direct. They kind of slid over to take me in and then dropped. I have an impression he was smoking a cigarette and that it dropped out of the corner of his mouth. But I'm not sure. Maybe it just seems to me now that he was the kind of man who would be smoking that way. Seems to me he was rather flashily dressed in a cheap way—in a light, striped suit, perhaps, though I'm not absolutely sure of that either."

"What about the other man—the one in the car opposite?"

"He had his back to me. I thought he rather hunched up.

29

He was heavy-set, I should say. Funny, but I remember I had a queer feeling that I had seen him before. Probably there's nothing to that, though."

"What was it about him that seemed familiar?"

"I don't know exactly. The way he crouched down. I can't remember who he reminded me of. I dare say I'm all wrong anyhow."

"Did you see him later down at the station?"

"I didn't have time to pick out any individuals. They were all shooting and they all came swarming forward."

"Notice the number of either of the cars or the make of the large one?"

"I did notice the number of the small car opposite the bank, but I don't recall it now. Seems to me the first two numbers were three and five, and that there were five numbers altogether."

"How did you happen to notice that? You don't remember the numbers of all the cars you see, do you?" asked the chief of city detectives with a manner that suggested suspicion.

"No. But I've been training myself to notice things. I thought if there was ever a hold-up it might be up to me to describe cars or people. So when I saw this putty-faced man go over and join the hunched-up one, after the fellow had lounged past and given me the once-over I stuck away the number of the car in my mind. I suppose they whacked it out of my head with their guns when they hit me."

"Do you mean you thought they were going to hold you up?" asked Burlson.

"Of course not. I mean that I had been trying to register in my memory anything out of the ordinary. For instance, if some ladies out shopping had passed, I wouldn't have noticed them. But these fellows hung around. I don't mean that they acted suspicious. I wasn't at all worried about them. I just noticed them."

"Natural enough," Carey said crisply. "That's what he was there for—to keep his eyes open." He added as an afterthought, "The girl on our switchboard remembers a hundred numbers of customers and firms with which we have dealings. It's the same principle."

"But you didn't notice the make of the other car?" Burlson said.

"No. I'm not an expert on cars, and it was probably forty or fifty yards from me. Besides, when I noticed about the first car I was standing around waiting for the shipment to be brought out of the bank. I had nothing else to do but look around. At the station I was watching the money and hadn't time to make outside observations."

Burlson nodded an admission of this point. He had not made up his mind about this guard entirely. He might have given the tip to the robbers and been shot by accident while pretending to exchange shots with them. The fact that they had beat him into unconsciousness later rather militated against this theory, but for a lot of money a man will take quite a hammering. Moran's defence of the shipment might be wholly a camouflage, designed to prevent suspicion from falling upon him.

The robbers had got away with a large enough haul to justify such a theory; to be exact, they had taken one hundred and ninety-two thousand three hundred and eighty-two dollars; for in addition to the weekly pay-roll at Petrolia, which was being sent to the leading bank in that town, a considerable sum was being transferred to pay for a transfer of some oil leases owned by an ignorant Bohemian who demanded cash for his property rather than a certified cheque.

Peter managed to catch Carey's eye before the banker and the detectives left. A wireless message passed between them. Carey was not sure what it meant, but he knew the young fellow wanted to talk with him alone. He left the hospital with the detectives, but separated from them at the entrance. He stepped into his own car, was run around the block by his chauffeur, and returned to Peter's room.

"Well," he said. "'What can I do for you?'"

"I'll be out of here in three or four days, Mr. Carey. I wish you would put me privately on this robbery case. I have a hunch I could help run down the robbers. Maybe I'm wrong about that, but I'd like to try."

Carey took a chair beside the bed. "Why do you think you could?"

"I've been following the case in the newspapers. My nurse has read to me all that has been in the papers. I had her get a back file. It doesn't seem to me that the police are getting very far with it, though of course they may be hiding what they have discovered in order not to alarm the bandits."

"No, I think you're right about the police, Moran. All their clues have come to nothing. They're up in the air."

"Well, I've a notion or two in the back of my head I'd like to try out if you don't mind letting me tackle the job."

"For instance?"

"I don't agree with the police that they've gone far from here. All this talk about their being in Cincinnati and Chicago and Atlanta seems to me just guesswork. And I don't think this is a band of famous crooks—at least not most of them. I think they are just amateurs. They will give themselves away; at least they would if there was anybody close enough to pick up the clues they drop."

"Where do you think they are? In Hilltown?"

"Maybe, but if I were on the case I'd spend a good deal of time at Petrolia. Birds of that kind flock where the pickings are good—and Petrolia is a wide-open town."

"There's something in that," Carey agreed, after consideration. "If you want to work on this as my personal representative, Moran, I'll be glad to have you. I don't mind telling you that this thing has got me. Of course we don't lose the money. We are protected by a bonding company. But in a sense it's a reflection on my management."

"Then you'd better not tell anybody I'm working on the case, or mention my point of view, sir. There's one thing you could have done, though. I'm convinced I'm right about the roadster. The number began with three and the second was five. There were five numbers in all. Get Mr. Burlson to check off every roadster in the city that has a license plate beginning with those two numbers—that is, every one with five figures. We may find out something that way. Another thing. The big car must be scarred with one or two of my bullet marks. Every private garage in the city ought to be visited, as well as the public ones. I'm convinced I hit one of the men. What became of him? What doctor attended him? Was the doctor paid so well for his silence that he kept quiet? If so, perhaps we can frighten him into coming to the police. Run a story in the papers saying that the doctor aiding the bandits is suspected by the police and is being watched. He may be so worried that he'll tell at once what we want to know."

"That's a good idea," Carey admitted. "I'll have that done. Anything else?"

"No, sir. Not till I am up myself. You'll let me know if the police pick up anything, sir, won't you?"

Carey assured him that he would.

CHAPTER VIII

Picking up Clues

Peter's suggestions to the banker stirred up at least a renewal of activity. The papers were still full of the bold daylight robbery. The reporters exercised their imaginations in suggesting ingenious theories most of which were cooked up while they smoked together in their room at police headquarters. They privately agreed, with the clever cocksureness of their craft, that the police were dumb-bells and that if they had been given a free hand they could have landed the robbers before this. But outside of newspaper speculation the policy of the authorities was mostly one of watchful waiting. They had rounded up dozens of suspicious characters and given them rigid cross-examinations. They had broadcast the news of the hold-up all over the country. All roads out of Hilltown were watched. But the officers had come to an *impasse*. The bandits apparently had left no trail behind them that could be followed.

Carey was a forceful man and one important in the community. When he called upon the Chief of Police the latter listened to him respectfully, even though with a slight irritation. The papers were beginning to criticize him for having failed to catch the robbers, and he was human enough to resent this.

"Of course that's been done already, Mr. Carey," he said. "I gave orders at once for all patrolmen to cover every garage, public or private, on their beats."

"And you found nothing?"

"Nothing. Inside of twelve hours I had a report from every sub-station in the city."

"Would you mind having it done again, Chief, as a special favour to me? The point is that if the robbers are local people——"

"But they're not. We're satisfied as to that. Blinky Craig's gang did this job."

"Very likely you're right, Chief. You know more about such things than I do. But we ought not to omit any chance.

33

Now if local people did so it those cars are probably in town right now. If so, they must be in some garage."

"Grant, for the sake of argument, that's true, Mr. Carey. Even if it was an outside job the cars are very likely here. But how are we to identify them?"

"I've just left Moran at the hospital. He's almost sure that the license plate of the roadster had five figures and that the first two numbers were three five."

"Well, that's something," the Chief admitted, "but not much. Of course they would change the license plate. That would be easily done just now because everybody in the city has to get a new plate this month for the new year. With forty thousand new plates being issued there would be no risk at all in getting one. Very likely they already had the second plate and substituted it immediately after the robbery."

"Then you can get at the Secretary of State's office the old and the new license numbers of all Ford roadsters whose last year license began with three five."

"All right. I'll do that," the Chief said.

"Another thing. Moran is almost sure he wounded one of the men in the small car, and he thinks his bullets must have struck the big one. If your men see a car scarred by bullets that would be worth investigating. Or if some doctor in town has attended a wounded man——"

"We've sent a letter to every doctor in town. Nothing doing. It's unlikely he hit any of the bandits. Naturally he was excited. At that distance he could not have struck anyone except by chance."

"It's possible Moran may have been mistaken when he thought he hit one," Carey conceded.

"Anyhow, I'll have a re-check of cars made, Mr. Carey, and I'll have the garages gone over again. To please you, because you've asked it," the Chief said, with a little emphasis on the words, "I'm not expecting to learn anything new."

Carey thought it as well to get a double check on the Ford roadster. He sent for Burlson and asked him to look up the owners of all the cars of that make which began with the numbers three five."

Before forty-eight hours Burlson came to Carey with news. He was a fat little man with a round, cherubic face. He looked like a guileless grocery clerk except when he remembered that he must be impressive and succeeded instead in being pompous.

"I've got it," he burst out triumphantly as soon as he was alone with Carey. "I've got the number of the roadster the robbers used, and I know who owns it. His name is Hilary Thomson. He's a plumber, and his shop is on East Twelfth Street. He's a perfectly respectable citizen, a church deacon, and he has a wife and three children."

"How did you find this out?"

"Began checking up the Ford roadsters the way I suggested to you. By and by I came to the one with the license plate 35444. The records showed who owns it. So I called him up. 'This Mr. Thomson?' I says. 'Yes,' he answers. 'You own a roadster with a license number 35444?' I says. 'Yes, have you found it?' he shoots back. 'Course I didn't give myself away, Just when did you lose it?' I asks. Right off the reel he answers, 'This afternoon of the eleventh—about two-thirty.'"

"Less than half an hour before the robbery took place," Carey said.

Burlson nodded, his little beady eyes shining. "I hiked right over to Mr. Thomson's place. He's all right, I guess. Anyhow, he looks straight. He reported his loss to the police that afternoon, I have found. The car was taken from in front of a barber's shop, where it was parked, while Thomson was upstairs in a rooming-house mending a leaky pipe."

"Of course that may just be his story."

"Far as I can I've checked it up. He did leave the car in front of the barber's shop and did some work on bathroom fixtures. The landlady sent for him. That's O.K. She confirms it, and so does the lady who has the room. She works in a beauty parlour, the woman who rents the room. I've seen her. She says she told the landlady the water in the bowl wouldn't drain without leaking a little and the landlady promised to get a plumber. When Thomson got through, he went downstairs and his car was gone. He went into the barber's shop and asked the barbers if they had seen anybody driving it away. The men in the shop confirm that.

"He seems to have a pretty good alibi. Yet the thing puzzles me a little. I can understand how the robbers might pick up a car for an hour while they needed it and then desert it after they were through. But the car hasn't been found. Evidently they still have it. Why should they keep a stolen roadster that may at any time get them into trouble?

"My theory is that they probably sold it to some farmer a few miles from town while they were making their get-away.

35

If the farmer had come forward with the car, he would have lost it; so he's hanging on to it in the hope that the identity of the car won't be discovered, and if it is he'll play innocent and say he doesn't read the papers much."

"Possibly," admitted Carey.

The banker submitted this theory to Peter.

"I suppose it's as good a guess as any other we're likely to make," that young man said. "The one thing we can be sure of is that if they have any sense they got rid of the car as soon as they could."

Peter left the hospital next day. Within two hours of that time he saw another of his suggestions bear startling results.

The Chief of Police had sent his chauffeur to bring Peter down to headquarters. The head of the plain-clothes department was not wholly satisfied that this young man was as innocent as he appeared and the Chief wanted to study the guard at first hand. So he put him through a quiz.

"Let's hear your story, son," he said.

The Chief had a way of calling all the young reporters "son," and he extended the term to include most of the men under forty that he met.

Peter told again what he knew. The Chief put some incisive questions. The plain-clothes department head had voiced a suspicion—it was hardly a suspicion, more like a remote possibility—that this young fellow Moran might be in with the gang, that in fact he might have organized the whole thing and tipped off to the others the best time for the raid.

While Peter was in the office of the Chief the desk sergeant hurried in bursting with news.

"I gotta see you alone, Chief," he said, with a glance at Peter.

The Chief followed him out of the room. He returned five minutes later.

"Come with me, son. I've got something interesting to show you," he said to Peter, and he reached for his hat and overcoat.

Peter donned his heavy overcoat. The weather was still bitterly cold.

They stepped through the outer office and the Chief stopped to leave some directions with the desk sergeant. Peter had no idea where they were going. He did not ask. For a moment it had crossed his mind that they might be arresting him, but he had dismissed this. The Chief did not have to leave his chair to have him arrested.

The chauffeur of the Chief's car drove them through South Hilltown, an old, rather *passé* residence section. An officer in uniform met them and was taken into the car. The Chief held a low-voiced conversation with him. Peter caught part of it.

". . . Just as you found it?" This from the Chief.

"Yes, sir. . . . Got Hamlin, left him there, and 'phoned to headquarters."

The next question did not reach Peter, but he caught part of the answer.

". . . An old stable used for a garage. . . . Window very high. . . . Nobody at home. . . . Found a ladder and looked in . . ."

"How did it happen you missed it before, when the first order was sent out?"

". . . My vacation. . . . New man substituting . . ."

The chauffeur, directed by the patrolman, swung into an alley and stopped at an old wooden stable. The men descended from the car and walked into the building. The Chief was just behind Peter. He was watching that young man closely.

What Peter saw was a roadster. In the seat beside the one behind the wheel a figure was huddled. Head and shoulder slumped back for support against the braces for the top. The coat was open, and the white shirt was stained just below the heart with a splash of red. This had been frozen stiff.

The Chief stepped forward and felt the body.

"Frozen," he said.

"From the coat pocket he drew a newspaper. It was dated January 11th.

"A *Post*, the early afternoon edition. Probably he bought it before the raid and had it with him," the Chief said. He swung round abruptly on Peter. "I guess you were right, son. You wounded him sure enough. Through the heart probably. The others left him right here in this garage and lit out."

Peter's blood chilled. He felt as though a block of ice were moving down his spine. He had killed this man. It gave him a shock.

"Recognize him? Ever see him before?" the Chief asked.

"No, sir."

"Well, he got his all right. He was asking for it." The Chief

37

glanced at the license plate on the car. The number was 35444. "It's the stolen roadster all right. It must have been lying here all the time. Someone is going to get into trouble about this." The last was fired in the general direction of the two patrolmen in uniform.

Peter knew that against this evidence the police could no longer harbour any suspicion that he had been in the conspiracy to raid the express shipment. It was possible that somebody in the bank might have given the bandits a tip but certainly that man would not have engaged in a battle with them, been wounded himself, and have killed one of the attackers.

Before Peter left, the Chief took occasion to pay him a compliment. "If you'd like to join the force, son, I dare say I could make a place for you."

The young man thanked him but shook his head. "It's the last kind of job I want. I hope I'll never have to fire a gun at a man as long as I live. I've had enough."

And he meant it. He had been on the side of law and order. What he had done had been necessary to protect the social order against destructive forces. He had to fire in self-defence, unless he had chosen instead to desert his post and run away. But the fact remained that he had killed a man, had struck out of life almost instantly a man who an instant before had been full of lusty energy. A wave of nausea swept over his stomach. He stepped out of the garage into the cold air and walked slowly toward the street car track.

CHAPTER IX

The Poker Game

Until recently Petrolia had been a country farming town named Centreville. It had gone its calm and rather sleepy way without any particular interest in stocks except as these reflected the price of wheat and cattle. On Saturdays the place had taken on a certain liveliness, due to the number of farmers and young people from the outlying country who had driven in to see a moving picture show or to eat ice-cream. But even the activity on that day had nothing feverish about it.

A change had come over the spirit of its dreams. Peter stepped off the train into a western town on the boom. Excitement, energy, bustle were in the air. The streets were crowded, so much so that many people were continually stepping off the sidewalks to get past. Loaded trucks rumbled along on their way to the oil-field. Houses and business blocks were going up by the score. On vacant lots tents had been pitched, and these flaunted pennants announcing themselves as restaurants, offices of brokers, and rooming houses. Stands had been run up for the sale of sandwiches and "hot dogs." In the air were sounds of hammer and saw, of snorting cars, of men's voices hawking wares.

Peter drifted along Main Street, carrying his suitcase with him, his eyes open for a place to put up. Men jostled him as they crowded past, not knowing he was there. The faces of most of them had a strained, nervous look. They were afraid that the fortune they saw just ahead might escape their grasp if they did not worry. It struck Peter that the atmosphere was unreal, feverish; that Petrolia was a gamble rather than a solid fact.

This sense of unreality increased in him after he had found a room and descended once more to the street. He dropped into the Stock Exchange and picked up snatches of talk in which dollars seemed to be counters rather than substantial realities.

". . . Cleaned up fifty thousand on P.P. and took a flier on Little Sister."

". . . Down three thousand feet. I'd ought to know tomorrow whether I'm a millionaire or a bum."

Peter passed two men near the door. One had the other buttonholed. ". . . A sure fire proposition, but I can't quite swing it myself. I'll let you in on a half interest for thirty thousand. Of course that's chicken feed, for such a gilt-edged lease, right up against the Johnnie K. But I'm kinda in a jam right now."

The other shook his head. "Looks good, Steve, but I haven't time to monkey with it. You'll make a big cleanup, but I'm too darned busy to know which way to turn, what with the Jack Pot Number Three coming in this week and——"

These men were roughly dressed, some of them unshaven. One of them he saw later waiting on the table at a restaurant.

Was this stage money they talked about so glibly or was he the only poverty-stricken man in camp?

At a lunch counter Peter fell into talk with a brown-faced youth who sat on the adjoining stool. He asked Peter to pass the salt and confided the information that this was a good hash-house to eat at. From this opening Peter presently learned that the youngster's name was Jim Dunn, that he had been punching cows in Montana until he had become bitten by the get-rich-quick microbe, and that he owned ten thousand shares in the Never Say Die and fifteen hundred in the Damfino.

They strolled out together into the roaring street. It was night and Petrolia had lit ten thousand lights and was devoting itself to hectic pleasure. Jazz bands tore the immense silence of the Rockies to shreds. Booted feet shuffled in crowded dance-halls. Saloons catered to customers with hardly a pretence of respecting the Volstead Act.

"Like to see the roulette wheel spin for a few whirls?" Dunn asked.

"Surest thing you know," Peter replied. "But I'm practically on my uppers. Not a bean to spend on the little round ball."

"That's all right. I know the guy who's doorkeeper at this joint. We don't have to play. They figure if we don't tonight we will some other night."

"I suppose the place is protected."

"Must be, don't you reckon? Somebody gets his rake-off all right. It's a block this-away an' a block up."

The gaming place was upstairs. They had to pass two doorkeepers before they were admitted. The first gave a signal to the second, who passed them on.

Peter found himself in a large room in which perhaps a hundred people were crowded. Some were constantly drifting in and out. About half of them were gathered round poker, roulette, and faro tables, playing the game of their choice. Others stood at the back of them and watched. Occasionally some player was cleaned out or cashed in his chips. Some one standing at the back of him at once slipped into the vacated chair.

The two young men loitered for a few minutes at the wheel. One pallid-faced gamer checked his plays in a little book. He was evidently using a system, as so many do at Monte Carlo.

Most of those about him made their bets more casually and almost at haphazard.

Moran and Dunn passed to the poker table. As they moved forward Peter's gaze fastened on a pair of heavy, rounded shoulders. There came over him a little shock of recognition. He had seen a pair very like them not long since hun hed over the wheel of a roadster. It had been his intention to stand behind them, but instead he circled the table so as to face the owner of the shoulders.

Some one began to deal and the man with the slouch looked up indifferently. His eyes met those of Peter. The man was Tim Murphy.

" 'Fraid Cat Moran!" he exclaimed, almost involuntarily.

"Peter Moran," corrected his former schoolmate.

Murphy accepted the amendment sulkily. Probably he remembered an unfortunate little episode in France. "That's what I meant to say."

He gathered up his cards, pinched them together, and slowly slid the edges apart.

"By me," he growled.

The second man passed, but the third opened the pot. When it came to his turn again Murphy backed in. After the draw the pot was raised. Murphy stayed, but at the second raise threw down his hand with a curse. From his pocket he drew a large roll of bills to buy more chips. He peeled off the two outside ones and tossed them to an attendant. Peter saw the denomination of one of them. It was a fifty. Evidently the game was not for small stakes.

Peter watched it, sizing up the players. There were six of them. The one to the right of Murphy was a big-framed outdoor man dressed in corduroys and boots laced to the calf. From appearance he might be guessed a well-driller, probably a contractor rather than a foreman. He played a liberal but a shrewd game. Next to him sat a cold-eyed, pallid man with a poker face, expressionless, merciless. Harrison the others called him. He was dressed in an expensive suit, but one a little too loud for good taste. A professional gambler, Peter guessed. To his right was a small, wizened man who might be anything inconspicuous from the proprietor of a shooting-gallery to a photographer. His name, it appeared, was Johnson. After Johnson came Butch Caraway, another professional gambler, Peter presently guessed. He was dressed as a cattleman and effected the bluff, hearty manner of one. The last man, the one on Murphy's left, was a youth who looked like a "lunger." They called him Bud.

Murphy had been the heaviest loser, with the possible exception of Johnson. As Peter watched the game he had a feeling that the dramatic pot of the evening had not yet appeared. If the two professional gamblers were in league there was no evidence of it. This was to be expected. Their work would not be coarse. They would not give themselves away, except so far as the play told its own story. Peter looked for gestures, words, ways of holding or laying down cigars, and knew quite well that if the two had a code he would not be able to interpret it.

Of course he might be all wrong. Harrison and Caraway might not be professionals. That was merely a guess, and he was helped to it by the way they handled their cards and chips, by the ruthlessness with which they cross-raised the coughing little consumptive out of a twenty-dollar pot which he lost the nerve to call when he had the best hand. Bud was living on a remittance from his people in Ohio, Jim Dunn whispered to Peter, and that he was probably playing his latest cheque. So far he had held his own, but he was a sheep ripe for the shearing and it was only a question of time till he would be cleaned out.

That is, if they decided it was worth while to clean him out. That would depend on whether they were playing for general results or for a specific end, in which latter case he could deduce that Tim Murphy's big roll would probably be the basis of attack. The two tinhorns might prefer, if they were playing for Tim, not to roil the waters until they had hooked and landed their big fish. A change in the personnel of the table was sometimes disturbing. Therefore they might prefer to let Bud stay. He was small fry anyhow.

Dunn was ready to move on. "Ready to go?" he asked.

"Just a minute."

Peter was watching intently a play that had come up. Bud opened a pot. His trembling fingers were a give-away to Peter. The boy had a good hand and could not control his excitement. Murphy dropped his cares. The man in corduroys did the same. Harrison stayed out. Johnson shoved in chips.

"The hide might as well go with the horns," he said. "Me, I haven't won a pot in an hour."

Butch Caraway met the bet and raised ten dollars. Bud hesitated. His black, shining eyes studied once more his cards. He hung for another moment in doubt, then raised twenty. Johnson rapped the table to show he was out.

Caraway laughed in the steel-trap manner of openhearted geniality he achieved in his role of cattleman.

"Looks like I stepped into something. Well, I'm aimin' to find out whether the boy's bluffin' or not." He raised the bet twenty more.

Once more Bud sat for a moment worrying. He had a ten full. From where he stood Peter had had a flash at it. The boy was not considering another raise. If he called and lost he would be broke, with no remittance for another two weeks. On the other hand——

He pushed his chips in for a call.

Caraway flung his hand into the discard with another laugh. "Caught without the goods," he explained. "Well, I always do bluff once in a game."

Bud raked in the pot, his hands shaking. He was nearly seventy dollars ahead of the game, and he had a queer feeling that it was by a fluke.

Peter had another view of it. He was convinced that this was "come-on-stuff." Caraway had advertised himself as a plunger, as a player who might draw to a flush, miss filling it, and bluff. Unless Peter was mistaken the real play of the night was now due, while the effect of this was still in the mind. There might be a little more skirmishing, but soon now the trap would be baited.

During the next round Caraway lost twice, rather heavily, to Harrison. Apparently he was still plunging, trying to win back what he had lost. He was building up the proper impression, and Peter reflected cynically that it was not costing him a cent if he and Harrison were partners.

It came Harrison's turn to deal. He dropped a card and stooped to get it. Peter stood motionless, eyes fixed, eager to miss nothing of what was to follow. This was crude, this dropping of a card in order to switch decks, but it was a simple method if one could get away with it.

Johnson opened, Caraway stayed, and Bud dropped his cards into the discard. Murphy raised, and the big contractor saw the raise.

"Got to hoist her again to keep the pikers out," Harrison said, and raised, pushing in a stack of five-dollar chips.

Johnson wrinkled up his wizened face. This was getting

steep. But he had a good hand, and three aces may easily become a full house. He stayed. Caraway also saw the raise.

Abruptly Murphy announced, "I'm playin' back, you understand."

"How much back?" demanded Harrison.

"My pile."

"Suits me," Harrison said. "Hop to it."

Murphy raised the pot fifty dollars.

"Count me out," the contractor announced. "I know when I've had enough, an' I don't mind tellin' the world that I'm laying down a mighty good hand." He showed to those behind him a queen high straight.

"High enough for me right now," Harrison said, counting out fifty dollars' worth of chips and pushing them forward.

"Too high for me," Johnson added, but he too met the raise.

Caraway woke up to take the play. "Hell, I've got some hand my own self. Kick her a hundred," he boomed.

Murphy's roll was on the table in front of him. He peeled off six fifties. "Didn't some one say something about keepin' pikers out?" he growled.

"I said that," Harrison said, looking hard at his cards, "and I'm wondering whether I'll have the darned fool luck to get the card I want. If I do—— Hmp!"

"You stayin'?" Murphy demanded.

"Wish I knew what you had, young fellow," Harrison replied. "Yes—yes, I'll see it."

Johnson felt very unhappy. There were better hands than his out, and he knew it. But he was in very deep, and if he happened to hook an ace or even a pair he would be sitting pretty. He could not drop out before the draw. But he availed himself of the player's usual privilege.

"I've got only forty-six dollars in chips left," he said. "Make yore bets on the side, gentlemen."

Harrison adjusted the pot, putting to one side chips to the value of three hundred and eight dollars. To this pile Caraway added two hundred, less forty-six which went into the general pot.

"Cards, gentlemen?" Harrison asked, picking up the deck.

Johnson took two, Caraway one, Murphy one. The dealer put down the deck.

"You standin' pat?" Caraway asked sharply.

"Why, yes. Thought I would." Without looking at his cards Harrison added another word. "Check."

"Same here," Johnson said. He had drawn a pair of deuces, but in any event he was out of the betting.

Caraway pinched his cards slowly apart, then counted out five hundred dollars in denominations of one hundred. Looking at Murphy, Peter could see that this gave him a mental jolt. For the first time it occurred to him that his hand might be beaten. Evidently the ex-service man had a very strong hand, but there are great possibilities in some one-card draws if the drawer holds the right combination to begin with. Murphy's thoughts could almost have been read aloud. What did this bet mean? Was Caraway bluffing, trying to drive the others out without a showdown? Or had he bettered his hand, made it impregnable? He might hold fours or even a straight flush. Or he might still be trying to bluff his way through.

Murphy called. Harrison threw his cards into the discard.

"Too stiff for me," he said. "I wish now I'd busted my flush and tried for a big hand."

Johnson spread his cards on the table face up. "Mine's an ace full. What does it get me?" he asked.

"It may get you second money," jeered Caraway. "Mine's a straight flush, queen high." He visibly crowed over Harrison. "I busted my flush, an' drew the jack of hearts."

Murphy stared at the five cards—the eight, nine, ten, jack, and queen of hearts. For a moment he sat there silent and motionless; then he ripped his cards in two and flung them away with a violent oath. He pushed back his chair, so that it fell to the ground.

"I've had enough of this damned game," he cried, and strode out of the room.

"Me, too," announced Johnson, rising.

It was the signal for the game to break up. The others cashed their chips.

"Wonder what Murphy had," the contractor said, and to satisfy his curiosity he gathered from the floor the ten torn pieces of cardboard. These he fitted into place on the table. Murphy had held four kings and an ace.

Moran and Dunn walked out of the rooms, downstairs, and into the blaring lights of the night.

"What did you think about that play?" Moran asked.

"I think that for a guy who plays as wild as Caraway he

was darned lucky," the cowboy answered. "Ain't that what you think?"

"Not exactly. I've got private notions of my own, and one of 'em is that a fellow who plays against Harrison and Caraway would be lucky to get out with his shirt on."

"You think the game was crooked?"

"Figure it out for yourself. Harrison dealt the hand. He helped Caraway cross-raise the pot. Murphy has four kings, and Caraway busts a flush to draw for a striaight flush—and gets it.

"Well, he was playing wild."

"Who against?"

"Why, against Harrison," Dunn said, after a moment's reflection. Then, after another pause while he mulled it over: "By George, do you reckon it could be that-away, like you think?"

"I could see it coming for ten minutes. Notice how Harrison dropped a card and stooped for it?"

"He switched decks, you think. By gosh, I'll bet he did."

They parted presently, Moran to go to his room. He had been watching more than a crooked card game. He knew that the money which had passed across the table from Murphy to the poker sharks belonged to the First National Bank of Hilltown.

Though he had no legal proof of it, he knew that he could put a finger on the first of the robbers. In the account book of his mind he wrote a number and a name.

It read: 1. Tim Murphy.

CHAPTER X

So Far, So Good. But What Next?

It was all very well to be sure in his own mind that Tim Murphy was one of the bandits. It was quite another thing to get legal proof of this. Unfortunately the bills of the express shipment had not been marked or their numbers taken. The fact that Murphy was playing a game far beyond his legitimate means was not evidence that he was gambling with stolen money. A good many men in camp had suddenly acquired great sums such as they had never in their lives possessed before. Such acquisitions of temporary wealth are incidents in the history of all boom camps. A man cannot be arrested, or at least convicted, on suspicion; and even if he could be the immediate result would be to drive the other robbers into flight.

The trouble was that it would be difficult to meet Murphy on a more friendly basis. The man had two grudges against him. He had wounded his vanity by publicly thrashing him and afterward saving his life. Both were offences which to a man of Tim Murphy's disposition were unforgivable. He was of a sour, grudging type. He had hated Peter when he had beaten him before their messmates, and he had hated him more when he had dragged him back to safety that day in the Argonne. It requires more generosity to receive a favour than to give one; and Tim was not generous.

Peter set himself to discover who Tim's associates were. He made inquiries, using Dunn to help him, though the cowboy had no idea that his new acquaintance was more than casually interested. Within twenty-four hours Peter knew that Tim Murphy was staying at a boarding-house run by a Mrs. Farrar. In less than half an hour from that time he was opening the gate and walking up to her porch.

A very pretty girl opened the door to his knock. She was soft-eyed and dark and slender and shy. Peter explained that he was looking for a place to board.

She shook her head. "Afraid we're full. I'll ask Mother."

Mrs. Farrar was a competent-looking woman, whose mind and thoughts were mainly occupied, he guessed, with the business of running a good boarding-house. She listened to what he had to say and began to explain that she really had all the boarders she could accommodate.

On occasion Peter's smile could be very winning. It was now.

"But you'll make a place for me, won't you, Mrs. Farrar?" he asked. "I want home cooking like yours. Restaurants suit some people, but they don't suit me. I've heard about your table. Naturally, I want to come here. If you want references——"

"I guess you're reference enough, young man. Do you want to room here too, or just board?"

"I'd like to room too, please."

"I don't see where I'd put you."

"The little sewing-room. Perhaps he wouldn't mind if it is a

47

small room, Mother," suggested the girl. "There's that bedstead in the barn, and we have a mattress for it."

"I'll bring the bedstead in and put it up myself," Peter volunteered. "I don't want to be any more trouble than I can help. It's good of you to take me. I appreciate it very much."

Mrs. Farrar had not said she would take him, but she gave in now. "All right. The room isn't much, but if you don't like it don't blame me."

Three hours later Peter had taken possession and installed his belongings. The room was clean, and when he had arrived the girl was arranging a cloth on the small table beneath the mirror. She brought in a waste-paper basket and set it beside the stand, and afterward an eiderdown coverlet for the bed. Each time she knocked at the door, though it was open, and waited for his invitation to come in.

"The blind doesn't work very well," she explained. "It won't go up. See."

He took it out of the socket, wound the spring, and put it back in place.

"Thank you," she said shyly. Then, as she beat a swift retreat, "Dinner is at six," she called back.

With him she left an impression of something more exquisite than mere prettiness, of a sweet and fragile personality, one that naturally appeals to the chivalrous instinct of men for protection. She had that most attractive charm, wistfulness. Very likely, he reflected, it had nothing to do with the quality of her inner life. It might be merely accidental. But it gave her a distinction, something that set her apart.

Peter was down to dinner on time. The boarders all sat at one long table over which Mrs. Farrar presided and her daughter waited on the guests. The food was good and well cooked.

The guests interested Peter. He checked off each one in his mind as they came in. There was a pert young stenographer of an oil company named Maisie. If she had another name Peter did not learn what it was during the meal because everybody called her by her first name. She was popular and slangy and quite able to take care of herself. There was an old bookkeeper who looked at the others over the rim of his glasses instead of through them. There was a nice young boy, a little bashful, called David Summers, who also worked for an oil company and was manifestly in love with Sid Farrar.

Also there were others whom Peter tabulated and put out of his mind as of no consequence to his plans.

Tim Murphy came in late. With him was a pallid youth whom Peter remembered instantly. He had last observed him slouching past the Hilltown First National Bank building toward a roadster on the other side of the street. His putty face and ferret eyes, a certain manner of furtive bravado, had registered themselves on Peter's mind. No doubt he had seen him later behind a gun at the station, but of that he had no recollection. He had then had no time to focalize faces.

At sight of Peter Tim stopped abruptly. Peter rose and offered his hand. Murphy took it sulkily because he did not know what else to do with it.

"Funny you're boarding here too," Peter said.

The other man—the one with the ferret eyes in the putty face—stared at Peter as though he were some one risen from the dead. His eyelids narrowed and slid away.

"Meet Mr. Hall," Murphy said out of the corner of his mouth. "Skate, this is Mr. Moran—served in France with him."

For a moment Hall's clammy hand rested in Peter's fingers. It was a good deal like a cold fish in the feel of it.

"Glameetin," the pallid man said, without looking at his new acquaintance. Peter translated the word, "Glad to meet him."

It occurred to him that he would not care to meet Mr. Hall in a dark alley if the latter had a grudge against him or knew that he was carrying money. Unless Peter did him gross injustice he was one of the new type of "bad man," a dope fiend who will do murder in cold blood without compunction.

Hall took a chair, slid one look at Mrs. Farrar's daughter, and appeared to devote his mind to food. Peter observed that Tim Murphy also glanced at Sid Farrar before he sat down. There was something in the quality of both these looks that disturbed him. She was a rare and lovely little flower, and men like these had no right to desire her covetously. There was something of desecration in it.

Moreover, he presently noticed something else, and this was even more disturbing. Sid was afraid of them. In the case of Murphy her eyes flashed a challenge denying her fear, but she never looked at Hall. She waited on him, her eyelids downcast, almost as a slave might serve her lord. Peter did

49

not understand it. Why should she fear either of these men? What could there be in common between this clean young thing and these two outlaws—one a ruffian, the other a rat from the underworld? It was as though they held something over her, as though she lived under the shadow of a threat.

Peter took occasion to finish his dinner at the same time as Tim Murphy. They met in the doorway, and he stepped aside to give Tim precedence.

"Hard luck last night," he said as they walked along the upstairs hall. "Some time I'd like to talk with you about that game. I'm no expert, but there was something about it didn't look just straight to me."

"What do you mean?" demanded Murphy, turning at his door.

"Maybe I'm wrong. Very likely I am. You're a lot better card-player than I. But I got a notion of a frame-up. I was on the outside, of course, and could see things better."

"A frame-up! Who rigged it?" Then, abruptly, he turned into his room. "Come in here a minute," he invited over his shoulder.

This was what Peter had hoped for. He followed into the room. Murphy closed the door.

"All right. Unload it. Let's hear what you suspect."

Peter told him and gave his reasons.

Murphy listened, sulkily but attentively.

"So you think they rimmed me?" he said at last.

"Card-sharps can rim anybody, no matter how good players they are, when they are not looking for crookedness."

"I don't remember Harrison dropping that card. But he did, you say?"

"Yes."

Murphy gnashed his teeth. "By God, if they did!" he cried, and slammed his fist down on the table.

There came a knock on the door, and at Tim's ungracious invitation it opened to let in Hall.

He stood, the cigarette drooping from a corner of his mouth, sliding eyes on Moran. Murphy rose.

"Much obliged," he said to Peter gruffly.

Peter understood that he had reached the limit of his welcome. He left.

The door had no sooner closed on him than Hall was catching nervously at Murphy's coat-lapels.

"Know who yore friend is, who you're entertaining, who you're inviting into yore room an' hobnobbing with?"

Tim shook him off impatiently. "Know him? Sure I know him. Went to school with him—served in the army with him. 'Fraid Cat Moran. That's who."

"You fool! He's the man who guarded the haul we took, the guy who killed poor Spike Slattery. That's who he is."

Murphy stared at him. The conviction broke on him that his confederate was right. He had seen the guard's name mentioned as Moran, but he had never associated the name with Peter. Why should he? So far as he knew 'Fraid Cat was a thousand miles away. And there are plenty of Morans.

But he knew now, by some instinct, that Peter had been the man. It was the sort of thing Peter would do—stand up and fire back while half a dozen men were shooting at him.

His eyes grew hard in reflection of his thoughts.

Meanwhile Peter was in his room next door making a second entry in the record of his memory.

It read: 2. Skate Hall.

CHAPTER XI

Peter Declares War

Alone in his room, Peter set himself to mull over the situation. He had made progress, decidedly; not through any skill of his own but by sheer luck. He had this advantage of the professional detectives, that he had been able to spot two of the bandits by recognizing them. But was it an advantage? How could he turn it to good account?

He had made an attempt to get into a more friendly relationship with Tim Murphy by warning him of the cardsharps. There was no valid reason why Tim should hate him. In their school days Tim had slammed him around a good deal. He had stopped that in France. Honours were easy. Later he had had the misfortune to do Tim a service by lugging him back to cover, but the fellow ought not to blame him for that. There had been nothing personal in it. Peter felt that he might have had a chance to wipe out, or at least diminish, the other's resentment if it had not been for this Skate Hall.

But he did not deceive himself. He had known in that instant when his eyes had met the startled ones of Hall in the dining-room, in that flash of time before the gaze of the putty-faced man had slid away, that he had been recognized as the guard of the express shipment.

Already this Skate Hall was busy obliterating any impression he might have made on Murphy. They would no doubt be asking each other what he was doing here? Why had he come to Petrolia? Why in particular to the boarding-house of Mrs. Farrar? Was he trailing them? Did he know they were two of the men who had attacked him? What did he intend to do about it? If he was a sleuth, what was the best way to circumvent him?

What immediate effect would Skate Hall's recognition of him have? Would all the robbers—all of them who were on the ground—at once decamp for San Francisco, Chicago, or some other remote spot? Or would they instead watch him and his actions, prepared to put him out of the way if their suspicious should become acute? This seemed more likely.

For there was one thing in Peter's favor. There had appeared in the Hilltown papers a little story—an inspired one of his own fabrication which reached the newspapers by an apparently careless mention of the fact by Carey to reporters —that he had been dropped from the pay-roll of the bank because its officials were not satisfied with his conduct as guard. The story went on to say that he had told so many conflicting details of the hold-up, that his accounts had so varied, as to give rise to a suspicion that he was holding back something. The papers had not said in so many words that he was suspected of complicity in the robbery. They left this to be inferred.

Peter knew that the bandits must have read this story. No doubt they read everything printed in each of the Hilltown papers on the subject of the raid on the van. They would do this in self-defence, watching for hints as to what the police were doing in the matter.

Naturally, then, if Peter was out of a job, he would drift to Petrolia. The place was a lodestone for all floaters within a radius of several hundred miles. It might be by sheer chance, so they would figure, that he had come to board with Mrs. Farrar.

He knew he was in danger, that he must watch his step

carefully, and the thought was not a comforting one. Petrolia was a camp rather than a small city in its point of view. A shot in the dark might finish him, and the inquiries that followed would be perfunctory. He could be murdered with a reasonable sense of immunity on the part of the killer.

While Peter lay on his bed in the darkness, face up toward the ceiling, there had penetrated to him sounds which at first he had not identified. They were smothered sounds, not loud, made by some one on the other side of the inner wall of his room. He listened. They were sobs, and they came from a woman or a girl rather than a child. He guessed that the girl was Sid Farrar. Probably she had the bedroom next to his. It was a small room, one of the sort likely to be reserved for one of the household when the best had to be rented.

Peter was sorry for her. He new that Sid was in trouble of some kind. But there was nothing he could do now. A man, a stranger, cannot intrude on a girl's tears, when she is in her own bedroom, to offer assistance which probably is not welcome. He made up his mind to be very considerate of her, to try to convey to her the feeling that he understood she was in deep waters and would help if called upon.

What could be disturbing her? Was she in love with one of these scoundrels? Murphy was a virile sort of ruffian. He might catch a girl's fancy. But where did Hall come in? And he could swear that it was Hall of whom she was most afraid.

He heard another sound—the turning of a doorknob; also the slight creak of a door, followed by a startled exclamation. There came to him the low murmur of a voice interrupted by protests, and hard on that a wailing "No—no—no!"

Peter listened, shamelessly, his ear close to the wall, all his senses attuned to tenseness. He could not make out the words, though he knew the murmur had grown more imperative, more insistent. There was the sound of a movement, other sounds which he interpreted as a little scuffle, then a voice in pain.

"Don't! You're hurting me!" it cried.

The listening man waited for no more. He slipped from his own room, opened the next door, and stepped inside.

In the room were two persons beside himself. One was Sid Farrar, the other Skate Hall. The man held the girl's wrist in his fingers and he was twisting her arm. An evil grin slit his lips.

At sound of the door opening he turned, then dropped the girl's arm and reached toward his hip. Peter had him by the throat before he could complete that gesture.

"You would, eh? cried Moran, and his fingers tightened. "You rat! You dirty little rat!"

Peter's other hand went round to Hall's hip pocket and drew from it an automatic. This he slipped into his coat pocket.

Hall's throat gurgled. He began to grow black in the face.

"You'll kill him," Sid cried, her little fists caught together in a gesture of distress.

"No fear. He's got nine lives, the vermin." But Peter loosened his grip and presently dropped his hand. With the fellow's automatic in his pocket he had drawn his teeth.

Hall collapsed into a chair and lay there coughing and clutching at his man-handled throat. He was at first beyond even curses.

"What's wrong? What was he trying to do?" Moran asked of the girl.

She opened her lips to speak, but she did not say anything. There had come a change over her face. She was again in the grip of that fear born of the fact that this Hall had some power over her. Her lips closed.

"It's—nothing. He was just annoying me," she said at last.

Peter smiled, the warm, friendly smile which carried with it comfort. "Let me be your friend, Miss Farrar," he said. "I'll see he doesn't annoy you again."

"No—no! It's all right," she insisted. Her haunted eyes denied the words.

"Nothing I'd like better than to show this fellow where he gets off. We'll have your mother chuck him out tonight."

"Oh, no—no! I don't want that," she cried. "Please, Mr. Moran, there isn't anything you can do. Nothing at all. Everything is all right. It is. It really is."

She pleaded with him as though she were afraid that by freeing her of this bit of humanity's scum he would wreck her life. Peter could not understand it. There was something back of it, something he could not get. It could not be that she loved, or ever had loved, Hall. The tie between them had nothing to do with affection. It was rather fear—stark, deadly, paralysing fear. But why—why—why? And if she was afraid why did she refuse his help, why decline to shift the burden to broader shoulders?

"But why not?`What are you afraid of? This fellow—there's no more substance to him than there is to an empty eggshell. We can crush him like—like that." His lean, nervous fingers closed strongly into a knotted fist.

"But no—no—I don't want you to interfere. Please, Mr. Moran."

"You're afraid of him. If you'll only tell me what it is——"

"No. It's all right. Really it is," she pleaded, and he could see that she was almost as much afraid of rash action on his part as she had been of Hall.

"He's got you scared. Forget it. He's not dangerous. Tell me what's wrong and I'll protect you. If I can't the law will."

Once more she broke into low-voiced protest, beseeching him to forget what he had seen.

Hall gathered himself from the chair and cast one sidling, venomous look at Peter. His fingers were still caressing his injured throat.

"One o' these days, right soon, it'll be you or me," he snarled. "I'll get you sure as you're a foot high."

He walked to the door and passed out. Peter had said he was not dangerous. But he knew that was not true. The fellow was more dangerous than a rattlesnake, for he had as few compunctions; but, unlike that reptile, would give no warning just before he struck.

"If you won't tell me, tell you mother what the trouble is," Peter pleaded. "You haven't got this thing right, whatever it is. You have no business having anything to do with that fellow—or Murphy either."

She sent a startled look toward him. "You—you're quite wrong," she said. "It's only that—he wants to pay me attentions—and I don't like him. That's all."

Peter knew this was not the truth, but obviously he could not tell her so. He repeated that she ought to go to her mother and put the situation up to her. "She'll give this fellow the right-about mighty promptly," he prophesied.

The girl shook her head. "No. I'm much obliged to you, Mr. Moran. It's good of you. But—I'm quite able to take care of myself. And I want you to promise me not to say anything to Mother. I don't want to worry her."

"I'll not promise that," he said, shaking his head, "unless you'll promise me something, that if he bothers you again you'll come straight to me."

"That's a bargain," she cried eagerly.

He had the uncomfortable conviction that he was pledged and she was not, for he did not believe that she would keep her word.

But he had done his best. There was no way to force her to give him her confidence. He turned to go.

She followed him toward the door, and laid her hand timidly on his coat-sleeve.

"You won't think I don't appreciate—what you did for me —and what you want to do? I—I think it's—sweet of you." Her voice broke. There were tears in her eyes.

"The best way to appreciate it is to accept my offer," he said.

"Oh, I will—I will—if I need any help," she promised.

And that, for whatever it might mean, much or little, he was forced to accept.

Peter was very careful how he left her room and passed into the passage. He did not want to stop a bullet while he was in the hall. After careful investigation he slipped out, stole to his own room, and whipped open the door, automatic in hand. Hall might be lurking in some dark corner ready to pour bullets into him as he appeared. He was very nervous as his fingers groped for the button that switched on the light.

He breathed a deep breath of relief when he looked round and found that he was alone and for the present safe.

Peter did not deceive himself. He had declared war upon this gangster personally as well as professionally. The fellow would call a conference of his confederates and they would take steps to get rid of him. That was certain, at least as certain as anything can be predicted in an uncertain world.

He knew that from this hour he was a marked man.

CHAPTER XII

Peter Puts Two and Two Together

Upon the door of Peter's room next morning there came a gentle tap. He was tying his four-in-hand at the time. Before he unlocked the door he slipped into his coat and dropped the automatic in the right-hand pocket. He unlocked the door with his left hand.

The young fellow David Summers was standing in the hall. He put his forefinger to his lips by way of caution.

Peter nodded silently and stood aside to let him enter. Then he closed and locked the door after him.

The clerk was a clean, good-looking lad, a blond with a clear complexion. Under the skin the warm blood came and went as it does in the cheeks of a young girl. He was saved from prettiness, from effeminacy, only by a certain quiet steadiness of the blue eyes.

"I wanted to see you, Mr. Moran," the boy said in a low, hurried voice, "because—because you look like a man to me."

Peter waited, without speaking. There is a strategic advantage, before a situation has developed, in letting the other party declare himself.

"And I've got a notion—I may be wrong of course—that you're the Moran who tried to fight off the robbers of the Hilltown First National Bank."

"Yes," admitted Peter.

The young clerk's voice dropped a note lower. "There's something hellish going on in this house. I know it. I can feel it. Yet I can't put just my finger on what it is."

"If I can help you——" Peter let it go at that. He wanted to convey to Summers an assurance that he was with him, but he did not want to direct in any way by suggestion the confidence he was about to receive.

"It's these two fellows that have come here to stay—this Murphy and that Hall. Ever since they came Sid has been different. She used to be care-free, the happiest kid I ever knew, always laughing, kinda from inside, as though she couldn't help it. We'd go out together and dance and have lots of fun. She just bubbled with life. Now—well, she acts as though she was afraid to be happy. Something is scaring her. That's how it looks to me."

"Have you any idea what it is that's scaring her?"

"I have an idea *who*. It's those two fellows—Murphy and Hall."

"How can they frighten her?"

"I don't know, unless——"

"Unless——" Peter stimulated.

"Unless it's about her brother."

"She has a brother then?"

"Yes, a wild young colt. It was through him that these two fellows first came here to board."

"When was that?" Peter asked.

"Well, they came first right after the Christmas holidays. They only stayed a few days then. Sid wasn't worrying about them any—not at that time. She didn't like them, and she let them know it. This Murphy tried hard to get her to go out with him. She went once, and after that turned him down cold. The other fellow didn't even get that far."

"Just when did they leave?"

"Well, let's see. They must have gone about the third or fourth of January. Earl went with them."

"Earl is the brother?"

"Yes. He came back a couple of days later and stuck around for a little while, then went back to Hilltown."

Peter felt that he was on the verge of a discovery, one that might reasonably explain why this girl cowered before these crooks.

He did not want to show undue eagerness, so he offered Summers a cigarette and lit one himself. He sat in the armchair, and flung a leg with obvious carelessness over the arm.

"When did he go to Hilltown?"

"I don't know the exact date. Let me see. It was near the beginning of a week. I remember that because he was packing when Sid and I came back from a Sunday picnic in the hills."

Peter took a look at the calendar. "Let's check this up. I don't know that it's important, but if we can find out when the little girl began to worry perhaps we can get at the cause. Was it the week of January eighth he left?"

Dave Summers wrinkled his brow in thought.

"Yes, on Monday of that week."

"That would be the ninth."

"Yes, if Monday is the ninth."

"When did he come back?"

"He didn't come back. He hasn't been here since."

"But—where is he? Isn't his mother worried?"

"If she is she doesn't show it. He's that way—a rover, always drifting away and never writing."

"He hasn't written either, then?"

"No."

It was as though Peter's warm, pulsating heart had been drenched with ice-cold water. Out of his sky the sun had suddenly vanished. Before his mind there appeared a picture—a flashing vision of a garage with a car in it, and in the car the huddled body of a dead youth, slain by a bullet from his revolver. He had to swallow once before he could ask his next question.

"What was Earl like? Describe him."

"Why, a slim young fellow, restless and high-strung, not easily controlled."

"I know, but——what does he look like?"

"Dark—black hair, and kinda tall."

Peter breathed again. He had not killed Sid Farrar's brother. The dead man in the car had been fair-haired, of the Scandinavian type, short and rather heavy set. It was very likely that the slain bandit had been some girl's brother, possibly some woman's lover or husband, but since Peter did not know the woman he escaped the shock of having dealt her a cruel and terrible blow.

"When did these two fellows come back?"

"Let's see. They've been here—— It was the twelfth they came back."

"And you noticed that Sid was troubled as soon as they got back?"

"Not right away. We went out to a movie that night, she and I. They came that afternoon while she was uptown, and when she got back they were settled in rooms. She did not like it, but they pay an awfully good price and I guess Mrs. Farrar hated to turn them down. I remember that night she was quite indignant about it. But when I came back from work next day she was changed. No fight in her—just like she is now."

"I suppose she and her brother quarrelled a good deal."

"They'd get furious at each other sometimes, but I never saw a brother and sister more fond of each other than those two. They are awfully close. It's funny too: wild as he is; he's just as devoted to her as she is to him. And that's saying a lot, for I think she'd do almost anything in the world for him."

The breakfast-gong sounded downstairs.

Summers got ready to leave. "What do you think about it?" he asked, his voice still low.

"I'll mull it over. Will these birds be down to breakfast?"

"Not likely. They never get up till about noon."

"I see. By the way, I'm looking for a job in town. If you can find me one——"

"Ever work in an oil-field? Our company is sinking a well. Maybe we could use you?"

"No experience," Peter admitted. "But I'd try to be handy

59

—if there's anything you could use a green man at. I'm a bit of an amateur carpenter—hammer and saw work, you understand. Nothing expert."

"I'll see what I can do. I'm interested in the company, so I can probably get a man on if we need another. We've lost a string of tools and are fishing for them right now. I'll talk with our driller today."

Peter walked down with Summers to breakfast. He thought he knew now why Sid Farrar was in the power of these men. Her brother was implicated in the express robbery and they were holding it over the girl. Peter had no intention of telling Summers what he suspected, but he meant to have a talk with Sid as soon as he could. He would break through her defences. After that she would have to accept him as an ally.

His chance came after breakfast. It was her duty to take care of the rooms. Peter intercepted her as she was about to start.

"Come into the parlour a minute," he told her.

She followed him listlessly. "There's no good saying anything more," she said.

He smiled. "Depends what I want to tell you, doesn't it? For instance, if I said I wanted to talk with you about your brother and these scoundrels you'd listen."

She flung a startled look at him. "I'll meet you in the clump of cottonwoods by the river in half an hour."

CHAPTER XIII

Under Cottonwoods

A lane beside the house led down to the cottonwoods, but Peter did not take it. He sauntered townward, quite well aware that the two gangsters might be watching him from a window of the boarding-house. In fact he went four blocks before he turned down a street that led to the river. Once at the stream, he retraced his way till he had reached the cottonwoods. Behind a large one he sat down and waited for Sid.

She was late for the appointment. When she arrived she came breathlessly upon him. She too had taken a round-about path.

"They've got binoculars," she said. "I was afraid they might watch and see I was meeting you. What is it you want to say, Mr. Moran—about my brother?"

He did not ask her why she was afraid they would see her with him if her story was true that she had nothing to fear from these men. Her words were a confession, but one which he had not needed to confirm his opinion. His desire was not to trap her into admissions, but to win her confidence.

"Just this, Miss Farrar. I know a great deal more about these men than you think. If I were to tell you something about myself would you respect my confidence? I've got to know before I go any further that it would be safe with you."

"Of course it would," she said indignantly.

"Ordinarily, yes. You are that kind of girl. But under the circumstances? You are afraid of these men. No, you needn't deny it. I know you are. The point is whether if you saw you had a chance, with my help, of freeing yourself from them and perhaps helping your brother at the same time you would line up with me."

She hesitated. It was quite clear that she was afraid of admitting too much and yet wanted to hear more. "I hate them," she said with a sudden intense passion of bitterness.

"You hate them, but you're afraid of them. I can tell you why. You think they have your brother in their power. If I convince you that this isn't true, that the only way to help your brother is to oppose them——"

"What do you mean—my brother in their power?" she asked, eyes fixed on him.

He brushed that aside. "Let's forget that for a moment, Miss Farrar. I'm offering you confidence for confidence. Do you want my help, my friendship—or do you prefer to live in terror of these scoundrels?"

"Oh, I want your help," she cried, and there was a little wail in her voice. "I don't know who you are, or how much you know. But you're good. I know that."

Peter did not argue that point. He knew his goodness was relative, but this was not the occasion for a discussion of abstract ethics. He held out his hand. "We're friends then—and partners?"

"Yes," she said simply.

"Good! To begin with, then, I'm the guard who, while defending the express shipment, was wounded by the Murphy-Hall gang."

Sid gasped. His abrupt disclosure caught her by surprise in

two ways: first, in that it told her who he was, and second by showing her he knew who they were. It was characteristic of her that she thought first of his safety.

"But if they find out who you are!" she exclaimed. "You don't know them. That Skate Hall!" She shuddered.

"I know them," he answered grimly. "And you need not worry about their finding out who I am. They know already."

"Then—what will they do?"

"Murder me, if they can do it safely."

"But you must go away. You must go today—now."

"No," he said.

"Why?" she demanded. "Of course you must. Why are you here? Don't you understand? There are others too here in town. They will kill you because of Spike Slattery. The newspapers said you—— Was it you?" Her dilated eyes were fixed on him in a sort of horror, while she flung the question.

"Yes," he answered. "It must have been, because I was the only one shooting at them. What should I have done—run away and let them loot the van?"

"What does that matter now?" She made a little gesture of impatience, almost of despair. "Don't you know that they will not rest, if you are here, until they have destroyed you?"

"Maybe, and maybe not. I'll be there at the time, you know, and I'll be very careful how I give them chances." He said it quietly, with an unperturbed manner that somehow gave her reassurance. This man was strong. His strength was not venomous, as was Skate Hall's, nor was it brutal like Tim Murphy's. It seemed to flow through him as a quiet, powerful river does through a placid meadow.

"Why are you here? Why must you stay?" she asked again.

"I'm here to bring those men to justice."

He saw her stiffen, could read the thoughts that raced through her mind. If he brought these men to justice, her brother too would be caught in the net. She was instantly in arms against him. He set about breaking down this new hostility.

His friendly, charming smile lit the man's eyes. "You're thinking about your brother now. And it's just here that you and I have to be frank with each other. You think he was in this job, that he had been led into it by these fellows. I don't think he was."

She clutched at this with swift, pathetic eagerness. "Why don't you think he was?"

"I have my reasons, and I'll tell 'em to you presently. But first give me your reasons why you think he was. Let's get all the facts before us."

"I didn't say I thought he was," she retorted defensively.

"No, but you do. Come, Miss Farrar, I've been frank. In a way I've put my life in your hands by telling you why I'm here. Isn't that evidence of good faith? How can I help you if you won't tell me what you know, if you continue to distrust me?"

She was silent, thinking, biting her lower lip.

"Even if your brother was led into this thing by these men, it's better to face the fact and see what we can do for him," he went on. "Give me your reasons for thinking he may have been in it, and I'll give mine for my opinion. Perhaps you are wrong. Perhaps I am. Let's weigh the evidence together."

Her anxious eyes again searched his face. She could read nothing in his clear, steadfast eyes but kindness and honesty.

"Why, everything," she replied, her voice breaking for an instant and then steadying. "He was with them. He went to Hilltown with them. He came back, but in a day or two left again. Then—there was the robbery. They came back without him."

"Without him—exactly. That's important. But let's clear up another point first. How do you know they were the bandits —this gang, I mean?"

"I found it out by accident. After they came back I went to fix the beds in their room. I thought they were out. So I used my house-key and walked in. I suppose I must have slipped the key in quietly and turned it quickly. Anyhow, they both jumped to their feet and faced me. They had guns in their hands and the table was just covered with bills and gold. Perhaps they thought the officers had come to get them. I started to go away, but they wouldn't let me. They made me come into the room and they locked the door again." The girl covered her face with her hands, trembling at the recollection of what had taken place.

"Yes," Peter said gently. "They bullied you, of course. They would."

"Yes, they threatened me with dreadful things, especially that Hall. He said he would cut my heart out if I told. But that wasn't the worst."

"No, the worst was that he said your brother was in the hold-up too. Isn't that it?"

63

"Yes, he said—and Tim Murphy said it too—that Earl was the one—the one who—who——"

She broke down and began to cry.

"The one who shot the driver. Is that what they said?"

"Yes," she sobbed.

"And that's all you know about it—what they told you?"

"Yes—except that since then both of them have been pestering me."

"Annoying you with love-making. Is that what you mean?"

"Yes." She went back to what was for her the more important issue. "Why do you think Earl wasn't in this, Mr. Moran?"

"I have two or three reasons. What Murphy and Hall told you has no weight. In the first place, they are liars; in the second place, they were caught with the goods and had to tell you a story that would insure your silence. What other thing would have had so much weight with you as your brother's safety?"

"Yes, but—— He had been with them for a week before the robbery."

"Then why didn't he come back here with them?"

"They said it was because he—he had shot that poor boy and had run away to escape arrest."

"Legally they all shot Bill. All of them were firing. How can they tell your brother did it, granting for the moment he was there?"

"I don't know, but they said so."

"They all made their get-away safely except the man in the roadster. Why should Earl confess guilt by running away when he wasn't suspected?"

And again she said, "I don't know." Then added, "But he did run away. He didn't come back."

"This isn't the first time he has gone from home and stayed, is it?"

"No, this is the fourth time."

"Was it usually when things were breaking in a way he didn't like?"

"Yes."

"Good! We'll suppose that Earl had got wind of what was afoot. Perhaps he had been approached to go in with the others on this robbery. He might even for a day or two have thought he would. But in the end he found he couldn't do it.

He is wild, say, but not a criminal. He had become involved with these men. He was afraid of their influence over him, and the pressure was strong because since they had told him of their plans they had to get him in for their own safety. So he lights out, we'll say—runs away—*the day before the* robbery."

"If we knew that!" she cried. "But we don't."

"But we do. At least we have good reason to think so. The police discovered, after the body was found in the garage, that the robbers had rented the garage for a month and the lower floor of the house on that lot. The people who own the house remember that one of the men—a young fellow whose description is like that of your brother—left early on the morning of the tenth with his suitcase. The man was watering his lawn when he saw this young chap slipping out. The police have found that he picked up a taxi at a stand two blocks from there and was taken to the station. It is believed he bought a ticket for Kansas City. If he did, and if he used that ticket, he could not have been in the robbery."

"Oh, if that's only true," the girl sobbed.

"One more point. I saw the robbers at close quarters. I don't think I would recognize them all again. But if one had been a boy like Earl I would have noticed it. He wasn't there, or I'm much mistaken."

"Are you saying that to comfort me?" she begged.

"I'm saying it because it's true."

"I'd be so happy if I could believe that."

"Believe it, then. I've a hunch that's just the way it was. Either your brother got cold feet at the last minute and ran away, or else—and this seems to me more likely—he was so young they didn't let him in on their real plans till they were all worked out. When they told him he was shocked, but he had trailed with them too far. Perhaps it came to a showdown. Hall and the others didn't just say so, but Earl read their minds and was frightened. He knew that if he didn't go in they wouldn't leave him alive to testify against them later. So he ran away. Maybe he left a note saying he would keep his mouth shut and stay hid for a while. Anyhow, they likely talked the thing over and decided to go ahead with the job."

"Earl isn't a criminal, Mr. Moran," she burst out. "He's not like these men. If you knew him—just a wild boy, but the kind you'd like. So dear, and so good."

"This may be the jolt that will save him. These fellows got hold of him and flattered him. Now he sees what they are really like he will very likely steady down."

"If he really isn't in it, if they don't send him to prison."

"I don't think they will. He may be innocent and yet a valuable witness. We must try to find him." He changed the subject. "What about the others who were in it with Hall and Murphy? I think you said that they are in town?"

"Of course I don't *know* that these other two were in the hold-up. These other two men—I think one is named Lynch and the other they called Tige—used to be with them all the time before the robbery when they were here in Petrolia. They would go up to the room Murphy had and have long talks, all of them speaking very low."

"Was Earl with them?"

"No, he had a job. But he'd be with them in the evenings. They were noisier then, though, and they didn't stay at home."

"Can you describe these men to me, this Lynch and this Tige?"

"Lynch is short and plump—that is, fat in a roly-poly way —and he always used to wear a hard felt hat, the kind they call a derby. But he doesn't now, for I saw him two days ago downtown. He had on a corduroy suit and a broad soft grey hat like the oil-men wear—only his are new and theirs are old and wrinkled and dusty."

"Anything more?"

"No, except that he talks a good deal and is quite polite."

"Good! And the other, the one they call Tige?"

"He's dark and lean, and his two front upper teeth are prominent. He's sort of slouchy in his dress. Oh, yes, and he chews tobacco. That's all I can think of about him."

"It's a good deal. By the way, about how old are they?"

"Lynch must be close to forty. He has a bald spot on the crown of his head. Tige is younger. Maybe he is twenty-five."

"Have you seen him in town since the robbery?"

"No."

"If you remember anything else about them will you tell me later? And don't ever speak to me while we are alone if there is a chance you may be seen. If they should suspect you actively you would be in constant danger. You'll be watched. So be very careful."

"Yes," the girl promised dutifully. She had accepted his leadership and no longer questioned it.

"They will quiz you about me probably. Stick to the attitude that I'm just a chance stranger of no importance in the situation."

"Yes," she said again; and then, just before she left, she broke out impulsively, "but you don't know how much better I feel. It's as though I had some one to lean on now. I'm not afraid—not nearly so much."

"That's right." He nodded cheerfully. "Now you'd better get home."

He noticed as she went that her step no longer dragged.

CHAPTER XIV

Peter Grins

It occurred to Peter, and not only by way of fleeting thought, that he had better share with Carey what he had discovered in regard to the express shipment bandits. His knowledge was too valuable to be confined to the brain of a man who might at any time be "bumped off," as Skate Hall would phrase it. Peter did not want to talk with the banker over the telephone. Operators have been known to talk, without meaning any harm in the world. Therefore he decided to run down to Hilltown on the inter-urban.

He looked up Jim Dunn first.

"Want to go down to Hilltown with me?" he asked. "We'll come back in the evening. My treat."

"Why, I don't mind if I do," the tanned ex-puncher said.

Peter was careful to be early at the inter-urban station. He was the first passenger on board after the door was opened and he took one of the rear seats. Jim sat down beside him.

"What's the big idea in squeezing past those ladies who wanted in?" the cowboy asked. "Afraid you weren't going to get a seat?"

"Afraid I wasn't going to get the one I wanted. I'll explain later—perhaps." He was not ready yet to tell Dunn that he would not have felt quite comfortable sitting in front of a man who had an ardent desire, one controlled only by the necessities of time and place, to shoot him through the back.

For out of the tail of his eye Peter had observed, trailing him to the station and later at the waiting-room window buying a ticket, a dark, lank, slouchy man with two prominent front teeth. He would have been willing to bet that his associates called this man Tige. Evidently the fellow's business for the day was to shadow him. The bandits were checking up information as to his habits and associates. They wanted to know where he went and with whom he talked.

It cannot be said for Peter that he enjoyed his situation. This was as bad as waiting for the zero hour. It was worse, for his enemies could choose time, place, and conditions. All the advantages of ambush and surprise lay with them. He had an imagination, and whenever he had wakened in the night there had jumped before him a picture of Peter Moran passing a dark alley or under an arc light or down a hall and suddenly crumpling up with a bullet through head or heart or spine; and each time the vision had brought with it a cold collapse of the stomach muscles. In the daytime it was better, but even in the sunshine he could find no enjoyment in the certainty that he was doomed for death, at least if these villains could make good their intent.

Peter took Dunn measurably into his confidence. "I'm in a hole, Jim," he explained. "That fellow two seats in front of us—the one sitting on the outside—is keeping tabs on me. Now I can't tell you the story yet because it's not my secret. But I'll say this much: I didn't bring you along just for your company. You can help me if you want to. I'll tell you frankly it may be dangerous. If you'd rather drop out of this thing I'll not criticize you. The car hasn't started yet. You can step off."

Dunn grinned. "An' me cravin' excitement like a range cow does salt! Oh, boy, I'm buyin' a stack of these danger chips right now an' sittin' in. What's the limit in this game?"

"The stakes are high and the limit is the sky," Peter answered gravely.

"Meanin' just what?"

"Meaning that I may be murdered within twenty-four hours. I can't tell you more than that."

The cowboy flung one startled look at him. Peter looked entirely serious. "Murdered! Say, boy, you kiddin' me?"

He half-expected Peter to smile, to admit that this was some kind of a joke. But no smile appeared. The steady eyes denied any humorous intent.

"I mean just exactly what I've said. There will probably be an attempt on my life today—if not today, then tomorrow."

The cow-puncher felt a lift of the spirits. This was what he had been looking for. This was high adventure sure enough. "I'm with you, boy, till the cows come home. What do you want me to do?"

"I'd like you to go to the First National Bank and ask for President Carey. Insist on seeing him. If necessary, write my name on a card and send it to him in a sealed envelope. Tell him I must see him at once if possible. Ask him to get into a taxi—not into his own car because I don't want it known who I am meeting—and to come to the corner of Thirteenth and Cheyenne Streets. You come with him."

"Sure. Anything else?"

"Notice this fellow in front of us. Every once in a while he turns his head to make sure I don't get off when the car stops. Size him up so you will know him again."

At the first stop in Hilltown, Peter said to Dunn, "See you later." He waited till the car was just starting then ran out to the platform and dropped to the ground.

A moment later another man appeared on the platform and descended hurriedly—so hurriedly that the momentum of the moving car sent him rolling in the dust. The man jumped up and looked around swiftly. His glance came to a halt at sight of Peter, standing a few yards away and smiling at him. He scowled, feeling no doubt rather sheepish. He had expected to see the man he was sleuthing on the run.

Peter said with mock politeness: "Hope you didn't hurt yourself. It's rather a good idea to get off before the car starts, don't you think?" He had waited to get another good look at the man standing.

The fellow glared at him savagely, but did not commit his opinion to words. Tige was not strong on repartee. His forte was action.

Briskly Peter stepped up the street. He hailed a tram-car and boarded it. Tige chased it and pulled himself on. He puffed from his run. Moran grinned. His grin expressed mock solicitude maliciously.

Twenty minutes later Peter descended from the car, followed by his shadow. He moved up the street as though headed for an immediate goal. Without looking back he knew that he was being followed once more. He heard behind him the slap of feet on the cement walk.

Suddenly Peter turned and retraced his steps, very slowly. Impishly he grinned as he met the other. Ten yards away he swung round quickly. Tige was turning at the same moment. Again Peter's quizzical smile mocked him as they passed. The man glared angrily. He did not enjoy being made a fool of, but his instructions did not cover this point. It was a possibility that had not been foreseen.

Peter hailed a taxi, jumped in, and said to the driver, "Lake Park." He looked through the rear window and saw that Tige was jumping into a yellow cab. The meter clock ticked up fifty cents, and Peter gave a second direction: "Back to where you picked me up."

He paid his bill and got out. When Tige left his yellow cab he saw Peter leaning against a lamp-post smoking a cigarette.

"Have a pleasant trip?" Peter asked blithely.

The outlaw glared at him sulkily. What was he to do or say? If it had been in a lonely spot, after dark—well, he would have known how to handle this situation. But in broad daylight, in the heart of a busy city, he dared not resort to gun-play.

Peter put his hands in his pockets, pleasantly at peace with the world, to all appearance at any rate. The bandit could only stand and glare at him fifty feet away. Tige felt like a fool. He did not enjoy being "made a monkey of," as he expressed it later to his companions. Awkwardly he waited, not knowing what else to do.

When the moment for action came, he was caught unprepared, through no fault of his own. A taxi rounded the corner and stopped in front of Peter. Inside it were two men and a woman. Peter opened the door and stepped in, and at once the machine started moving.

Instantly Tige wakened to action. He looked around hurriedly for another cab. None was in sight. He turned and began to run after the car. Presently he stopped. It was drawing away from him.

CHAPTER XV

A Conference in a Cab

The two men in the cab were Carey and Dunn. The woman was Janet Carey. At sight of her Peter looked his surprise but asked no question.

"I was in the office with Dad when your friend arrived, and made him bring me," she said by way of explanation.

To Carey, Peter said with a smile, indicating the man running after the car, "Like to stop and pick up our anxious friend? I've a notion you might like to meet him."

"Who is he?" the banker asked.

"They call him Tige. He's one of the men who robbed your bank."

Carey looked at him. "What?" he snapped.

Janet said nothing, but her eyes began to sparkle.

Peter nodded. "Fact, Mr. Carey. He's one of them."

"You're not joking, young man?"

"Not so you can notice it," Peter answered grimly.

"I should think he'd be the one running away and not us," Janet put in.

"Give us the answer to your conundrum, Moran," the banker said.

"I came down today to tell you what I've found out. That's part of it, that this fellow is one of the robbers. He's been sent to Hilltown as a delicate attention to me. They want to find out who I see and talk with and what I do. They are interested because they know I know."

"Know what? What do you know?" demanded Carey.

"I know the four men who robbed the van and where two of them are rooming. As a matter of fact, I'm staying in the same house, next room to theirs."

Janet opened her brown eyes to their widest. "But is that safe, since they know who you are?" She answered herself at once. "It can't be."

"I've had notions along that line myself," Peter agreed.

"It's not a very safe game I'm playing. That's why I ran down to have a talk with Mr. Carey."

The young woman frowned at him anxiously. "If they

know you know them—that they are the robbers, I mean—they'll stick at nothing, Peter. It's lucky you got away alive."

"Yes, but I'm going back today. That's why I had to get in touch with you, Mr. Carey. So that you would know what I do if anything should happen to me."

The banker looked sharply at him. "You're not expecting anything to happen to you, are you?"

"Not if I can prevent it. But there's no use in not facing the probabilities. I'm expecting that if they get a chance they will try to murder me inside of forty-eight hours."

He said it quietly enough, almost casually, but the heart of the young woman seemed to turn over. The eyes that looked at him were fear-filled.

"Tell us your story, Peter," the banker said.

"First, let me introduce to you Mr. Dunn. If you've no objection I want to take him in with us. I may need help."

At their first meeting Carey had sized up the tanned young cow-puncher. The boy's face was a letter of recommendation. In the bulk of his shoulders there was the promise of strength.

"Suits me if it does you, Moran. You're in charge of field-operations. Now let's have your story."

"Just one thing before I begin," Peter said, turning to Dunn. "There's still time for you to drop out of this, Jim. I don't want to take advantage of your good-nature to ring you in on anything you'd rather keep out of. This business is mighty serious. It may mean the difference between life and death. These fellows won't stick a moment at murder if it suits them."

Dunn's white-toothed grin was reassuring. "I was a kid when you fellows had that war in France. Seems like to me I never do get in anything good. I'm always just too soon or just too late. Lead me to this little private war of yours, I'm in."

"Remember one thing, Dunn," Carey admonished. "From what Peter says I judge this is dangerous work. You mustn't do any talking outside."

"I'm a clam," the cowboy promised.

"Good! Now for your story, Peter."

Peter told it, taking care to keep his voice down so that not a word of it could reach the driver of the taxi through the glass. Those in the cab with him listened intently while he told his story. When he came to the account of the card-game Carey raised a point.

"What about these other fellows—the two professional gamblers? Do you think they are in the robbery at all?"

"No, I don't think so. Tinhorn gamblers always flock to boom towns. I followed the game closely because it gave me a line on Murphy and his roll of bills and because I wanted to find out if I could whether any of the other players were friends of his."

"And you think they weren't?"

"Yes, I thought he was playing a lone hand."

Peter went on with his story, telling how he had used the game to give him a chance to renew his acquaintance with Tim Murphy later. He told what followed, his difficulty with Hall, and his conversations with Sid Farrar and David Summers.

When he finished speaking the banker made one appreciative comment. "Well, you've done better than the whole police and detective force of Hilltown. You've got the right men located, I judge."

Janet was more impulsive in her congratulations. "I think it's wonderful what you've done. You've only been out of the hospital about two days and already you've got the whole gang."

The young man flushed. "I haven't got them, Miss Carey. The real job lies before us. I've had luck and special advantages the police didn't have. I was able to recognize two of the men when I saw them, and Miss Farrar and her young friend gave me help. But so far we've only made a good start. The point is to round up the crooks with evidence enough to convict."

"Haven't you evidence enough?" asked Dunn. "Seems to me you've got 'em sewed up. You testify you recognize the birds, Miss Farrar says they told her they did it. When you arrest 'em you find the money——"

"The numbers of the bills weren't taken and the money can't be identified," Peter said. "Besides, we haven't anything at all yet on Lynch and Tige. We've got to tie them up with the robbery as well as the others."

"That's up to the police, I should think," Janet protested. "They can surely do something, if they're any good at all. I suppose you're going to tell us now that when you've escaped from those villains alive you've got to go back and let them shoot you. It would be ridiculous, if it weren't so serious."

"Yes, I've got to go back," Peter said. "I've set my hand to

73

the plough, and that sort of thing. I came down to get Mr. Carey's advice. When you say turn the whole thing over to the police—why, it's not quite so simple as that. For one thing, as I said, we've got to get evidence connecting them all with it. We have to protect Sid Farrar. We have to find her brother and use him as a witness. Of course we can do that later. The point is that the police are likely to blunder in, giving them the chance to destroy evidence and to slip out of the net we're weaving around them."

"Yes," agreed Carey reflectively. "Yet, after all, the arrests are a police job. We'll have to trust them. I'll drive up to Petrolia tonight with Burlson and see the Chief of Police there. Before I tell too much I'll size him up."

"All right, sir. Jim and I will try to find out where the other two men are stopping. We'll all have to move very carefully. The least slip may send them flying away, because by this time they are probably pretty well alarmed. They very likely think there is a net of detectives all round them. Don't you think we ought to have them shadowed—those of them we know how to reach?" Peter asked.

"Yes. I'll arrange for that. I'll have Burlson take up some of his men and put them on the job."

They talked the thing out at length, arranging details as far as they could.

"Are you both armed?" Carey asked before they parted.

"I'm not," Dunn answered. "Left my six-gun at the ranch."

"You'd better get a good revolver, the kind you like best. What will it cost?"

The cow-puncher made an estimate and Carey gave him money. He also handed Peter a small roll of bills. "You may have expenses you don't figure on," he said.

After the taxi had returned to the business section of the city, the young men descended from it.

"Peter," called Janet in a low voice.

Moran came round to her side of the car.

"I don't think you have any business going back up there. It's tempting Providence. But if you must go you'll take care of yourself, won't you?"

"Yes."

"You'll not be reckless, will you? Promise me that."

"I'll promise that, Miss Carey," he said promptly. "I'm not anxious to be shot, so I'll not throw down on myself, as Jim puts it."

"We-ell——" she said reluctantly, not at all satisfied. Then she added, without apparent relevance, "Why don't you call me Janet? You went to school with me."

"All right, Janet."

Still she could not bring herself to let him go. The colour deepened in her cheeks. "I don't think you ought to go back, Peter. It isn't worth it, even if they do escape. It's not your job now. Let someone go they don't know. Why, they'll be waiting for you. No sense in walking into an ambush with your eyes open. I'd call it just foolhardiness."

"Nobody else knows them. No, if I didn't show up they would light out tonight. As long as I'm on the ground they won't be so anxious to go, because they can watch me. Anyhow, I've got to go through."

There was nothing more to be said. She knew she could not move him from his decision to return to Petrolia, and as long as he was in the oil town with the bandits free he would be in imminent danger. But she could not sit down in Hilltown with her hands folded and await the issue. The hours would be torture. She said as much to her father when they were alone.

"Sorry, Janet," he said, "but it can't be helped."

"I'm going with you," she said.

He shook his head. "No. I don't know that there is any danger, but there might be. If you went you would have to stay in an hotel there and wait for me. What advantage would that be?"

"I'd be nearer. Let me go, Dad," she urged.

"What would your mother say?"

"She needn't know. You'll just say you're going to Petrolia on business and may be away all night."

Her father did not argue with her further. He liked the spirit of his slim, impulsive daughter who identified herself so completely with his interests. It did not occur to him that the cause of her imperative urge to get close to the scene of action lay in her interest in another man.

"I don't suppose there is any real danger. In fact, I don't see how there can be. But if I let you go you'll have to promise to do exactly as I say."

Janet promised. She would have promised anything just now to get what she wanted.

Peter appealed to her imagination as no other man ever had. All the boys in her set at college had been more or less alike, cast in the conventionalized mould made by the little world in which they moved. The same had been true of the men who belonged to her social world. They conformed to type. Except in small ways they had not enough freedom of mind to break through the hedges of custom built around them. Peter was different, more of an individual. She had had visions of knowing men like him——men who did things other than the ones everybody else did, and who did them in an interesting way. But she had almost given up expecting to meet any until Peter had come within the orbit of her vision.

It was not, after all, so much what Peter had done. He had achieved no visible success that one could put a finger on. He had built no bridges across impassable gorges in the Andes, had won no crown of glory as an explorer. It was rather what he was.

She liked him for himself. She liked his friendly, whimsical smile, his little manner of modest self-depreciation, the courage with which he set his teeth into a job. Also, she liked his fine eyes and his strong white teeth and various other personal assets he possessed.

Janet wished that Jack had enough imagination not to be so stodgy. He didn't like Peter, and she told herself it was because he had not enough vision to appreciate him. Which perhaps was not quite fair to Jack. His chief reason for disliking Peter was that a true instinct told him that the man was dangerous, one who might very easily balk a project at present much on his mind. He knew how impressible Janet was, how impulsively she gave herself in friendship. His failure to share Janet's enthusiasm about Peter was quite well justified.

CHAPTER XVI

A Find

Peter took the precaution to slip into the house by the back door. The outlaws might be watching for him. If so, it was just as well to approach unexpectedly from the rear.

Mrs. Farrar looked a little surprised to see him step into the kitchen. He had not struck her as the sort of young man to make himself too free—not at all as impudent as some of her other boarders.

He apologized. "My feet were a little muddy so I cleaned

them back here," he explained. "May I go up the back stairway?"

This was a motive Mrs. Farrar could appreciate.

"Of course. It's raining hard, isn't it? Quite a change in the weather. I like it better than that we've been having. Too cold for me."

Peter agreed. He went upstairs noiselessly. It was possible the bandits might be lying in wait for him—possible, but hardly likely, since the odds were that they would not move against him till night. From the stairs below the landing he peered along the hall, then tiptoed to his room, unlocked the door, and went in.

An idea had been developing in his mind. It had occurred to him first on the inter-urban during the ride back. Why wait for the enemy to attack? Why not go into their territory and see if he could pick up any evidence connecting them with the robbery? It had seemed on the whole a feasible proposition and he had stopped at a locksmith's and obtained a bunch of keys.

He opened the door of his room a little and listened. Unless they were asleep he was convinced the outlaws were not in their room. There had come from it no sound whatever, nor did he hear any now. They usually were out in the afternoon. No doubt they were today.

Peter removed his shoes, stepped into the hall, and moved down it to the door of the next room. The doors at Mrs. Farrar's house had the ordinary keys and locks used in old-fashioned houses. The locks were the kind that could be opened by a skeleton key of the same general make.

He tired the keys, one after another, working with the greatest caution to avoid making a noise; for he knew that if one of the bandits were at home and awake there would instantly be trouble serious and explosive. Very gently his fingers inserted the keys and turned them as far as he could. The fifth one he tried went round smoothly without any difficulty.

Peter slipped the keys back in his pocket, put his hand on the butt of his Colt, and opened the door quietly. One glance told him that there was nobody in the room.

He looked around, uncertain where to begin his search. There was no way of telling when Murphy or Hall, or both of them, might return. Therefore he could afford to lose no time.

His first thought was of papers, letters, or notes that might have a bearing on the case. The table drew his eye. It was littered with all the objects that clutter any receiving space in the bedroom of untidy men. There were broken cigars, a package of cigarettes, matches, cards, a razor-strop, shaving cream, a cheap magazine, and several more or less empty glasses smelling of bad gin. There were no letters.

Nor did the drawers hold any papers of interest except the receipt for a month's rent signed by the man in Hilltown where they had stayed prior to the robbery. This Peter slipped into his pocket.

In five minutes he had made a swift, cursory examination of the room, and except for his first find had discovered nothing. He stopped beside the bed for a moment to consider the situation. It was likely that some of the stolen money was here in the room. Each man could not carry his share about with him all the time. If the amount taken had been divided into four parts this would run to more than forty-five thousand dollars each. Part of it was in silver—at least three thousand dollars. Men of this kidney did not trust each other any further than they had to do. Therefore they had not buried it all in the same place. They dared not put it in a bank or even in a safety deposit box because it would have to be handy at any hour of the day or night in case of a forced sudden getaway. Logically then a large part of the share of Murphy and Hall ought to be on the premises, and in this room by all the laws of probability. Where? Inside the mattresses? The bills possibly might be there, though that was an old device.

Still, one never could tell how the minds of men like these two would work. The chances were that they changed the hiding-place from time to time. Peter pulled the covers from the bed and made a careful examination of the mattress. There was no evidence that it had been tampered with, though he looked at the seams to see if they had been recently opened. Peter remade the bed.

The clothes closet attracted him next. He had already been through the pockets of two old suits hanging there. Now he dragged out these, two overcoats, and two pairs of shoes. These last were as heavy as though weighted with lead. Peter knew at once that he had found some of the treasure. He tilted forward one shoe and a pile of silver dollars rolled out. Below there were cartons evidently packed with silver of the same denomination. In the closet he also found a brown bag of imitation alligator leather. This was empty. Without giving the matter further thought Peter emptied the contents of the shoes into this bag.

As he stepped back from the clothes closet Peter's stockinged feet became sensible of a softness in the carpet where he was standing. He looked down and saw that it was raised here somewhat above the surrounding level of the rug.

He knelt and gave a little tug at the corner of the carpet. The brass-headed tacks that held it came up without resistance. Beneath the rug, arranged in layers, were rows and rows of bank-bills.

At that inopportune moment Peter heard something that brought him rigid alertness. It was the heavy, growling voice of Tim Murphy. The sound came from the foot of the stairs.

Peter had no time to think out the best course for him to pursue. He snatched up the bills and crammed them into the suitcase, then dropped back the rug and flung the shoes into the closet. Swiftly he padded to the door, carrying the bag with him in one hand, his revolver in the other. He put the bag down and opened the door.

The sound of Murphy's voice still came booming up the stairs. He was talking with Sid Farrar. Hall's whine also reached him. The men were beginning to ascend the stairway. Peter locked the door, caught up the bag, ran swiftly to his own room, and entered. He locked and bolted the door behind him.

Already Peter knew that he had made a mistake—a very serious one. He should have left the money where it was. They would miss it, almost at once. This would either precipitate a battle or drive them to flight. But it was too late now to amend the error he had made. The bandits were already entering their room.

Peter knew he must get rid of that bag at once. There would be no chance now to walk out of the house with it and make good his escape. He was caught. A sudden oath from the next room told him that the loss had been discovered.

He walked to the window and raised it as noiselessly as he could. It was raining dismally outside from a sodden sky. Already darkness of early winter was beginning to fall. Below him and a little to the right was a water barrel put there to catch the rain from the eaves. It was full. He leaned out, caught hold of the big wistaria vine that ran past his window, and with a swing dropped the brown bag plump into the water barrel. It sank like a plummet, splashing water in every direction.

It was time that he should also vanish. Excited voices came to him, explosive oaths. A door banged open. There was a rush of hurried footsteps and the rattle of a fist banging at his door. The knob rattled. A heavy voice demanded with a curse that he open the door and let them in.

He heard Hall's voice. "He's in. See, the door's bolted."

"Sure he's in." Murphy's growl reached the man inside. "We know you're there. If you don't open——"

Peter gave no answer. He was considering ways and means. They would presently break in. Then somebody would be killed.

The door quivered with the shock of a heavy body flung against it.

By this time Peter knew what he meant to do. He slipped the gun in his pocket and soft-footed to the window. In a moment he was astride the sill and reaching for the thick trunk vine of the wistaria.

There came another crash, the sound of splintering wood. Then a third and a fourth.

In another moment they would be inside. Peter slid down part of the way and lowered himself from hand to hand. As his feet touched ground he looked up. Murphy was leaning out of the window and behind him was Hall's white, malevolent face. In that instant, before Peter had time to turn, the pallid gangster's automatic barked twice at him. He heard it again as he dived through the rain into the wet bushes and from them dodged around the corner of the house.

Peter's heart pounded like a throbbing engine as he raced into the darkness of the gathering gloom. He sped down the path in front of the house to the sidewalk, swung to the right, and flew forward like a halfback on a football field carrying the ball. A queer, panicky feeling surged up in him. He could only think of putting distance between him and that automatic which had been spitting bullets at him. If he had stayed in his room two seconds longer somebody—perhaps all three of them—would by now be lying dead or dying on the floor. At that distance, practically within arm's reach of each other, some of the stabbing shots would have found vital spots.

His pace slackened. He could hear no sound of pursuing footsteps. Indeed, when he came to reason calmly, he realized that he had too good a start to be caught. It was just as well to go a little easier. Two or three men and a couple of young girls, returning from work, took in with evident astonishment the sight of a man, hatless and shoeless, flying through the rain at such a pace. Word might be passed around that a madman had escaped. At more than one dinner-table a strange story might be told that night.

He took a side street, heading for the rooming-house where Jim Dunn stayed. The driving rain beat on his face and bare head. His socks squashed water at each step, and when he reached the rooming-house they left soggy tracks on the porch and stairs as he ascended. Fortunately he reached his friend's room without having met anybody in the house.

Jim was at home and answered his knock with a "Who's there?" Since he had become involved in the business of running criminals to earth, the cow-puncher had learned to be a little cautious about flinging open his door to chance callers. Peter's voice brought him at once to the door.

His coat was off and his shirt-sleeves rolled up from the muscular forearms. A towel was in his hand. Evidently he had been washing prior to stepping out for dinner. He stared at Peter in amazement.

"Say, old Hellamile," he got out at last, "since when have you started this here back-to-nature stunt of trailin' through the rain without yore boots an' sombrero on?"

"Since Skate Hall started potting at me with an automatic while I'm shinning down a wistaria vine," Peter answered. "Got any socks to loan me, Jim? Mine are a little moist."

"Socks? Surest thing you know." The ex-cowboy rummaged through a drawer to find a pair without holes and flung two grey woolen ones at him. "But what's this stuff you're pullin' about the wistaria vine an' Hall?"

"No fairy tale," Peter replied, stripping from his feet the sodden socks.

"Onload yore tale of woe, boy," Jim said, manifestly excited, though he tried to keep his voice indifferent and casual.

Peter told the story, but he omitted certain parts of it. He did not mention that he had left that part of the stolen money which he had recovered in a rainwater barrel.

The narrative filled young Dunn with gloomy lament. He

smoked a cigarette dolefully. "Lordy, an' me not there. I never am. I'm one of these here alibi birds, always round the corner when anything live is happenin'. I'll bet I don't get in on a thing during this whole darned show. You'll hog it all. Why didn't I trail along with you to yore place like I had a notion to? Now, why didn't I? Can you tell me that?"

Peter washed his feet and put on the dry socks. "You can have my seat at the front any time the fireworks begin to play, Jim. I've had excitement enough to last me a lifetime. I don't like it—not a little bit. All my life I've been a quiet chap, not looking for trouble, and it always seems to be camping on my doorstep. My hair will turn grey if this thing doesn't stop. I'm a timid fellow and I don't enjoy being potted at. You should have seen me go like a blue streak. I ran like a scared pup."

"Aw, hell! You can't pull that line on me, boy. You're one of these eat-'em-alive birds. But, say, what's gonna happen now? Those guys must know it's gettin' right close to a show-down. What'll be their next play?"

"That's what I'm wondering, Jim. Aren't they likely to figure that I've got some friends and we're trying to high-jack them? Won't they think that if I was in with the police, officers would have searched the room? If they do, if they get a notion that this is a private job on the part of some of us to skin off some of the cream of their robbery, why, they'll stay to try to recover what I got from them. Even if they suspect they are being shadowed by officers they will hate to give up all that silver and currency I recovered from them."

"Say, where is that dough?" Dunn asked. "You didn't bring it with you, did you?"

"No, they were too hot on my trail."

"Didn't drop it on the way, did you?"

"Yes." Peter's eyes danced. "I did just that."

"Say, we'd better hike back, boy, an' get it. Right now, *pronto, toute suite,* immediately, if not sooner."

Peter affected a manner of careless indifference. "Oh, I reckon there's no hurry. It'll be there when we want it."

The cowboy was puzzled. "What makes you so darned sure? You in the habit of leaving twenty or thirty thousand dollars lying around loose that-away?"

"No, I wouldn't call it a habit. But you see I put this in a safety deposit box."

"That's different." Again another aspect of the situation struck Jim. "What did the bank clerks say when you hot-footed in without any hat or shoes? An' do the banks in this burgh stay open till half-past five?"

"This was a private safety deposit vault. I'll show it to you later." Peter deflected the conversation. "You'll have to bring me back some sandwiches. They'll be hunting the town for me likely, and I don't want to meet them just now. I wouldn't show myself very prominently if I were you, Jim. That fellow Tige knows you."

"I'll kinda melt into the scenery inconspicuous like a ptarmigan does," Dunn promised.

When he had fitted his tie to his satisfaction he went out gaily in the hope of an adventure. He had promised not to go looking for one, but if one looked for him he could not be blamed.

Left to himself, Peter reflected ruefully that he had spilled the beans. If the bandits decamped hurriedly it would be his fault. He ought never to have taken the money from their room. But he had been caught by surprise, given not an instant for reflection, and he had followed the impulse of the moment. Well, it could not be helped now, though, of course, the police would blame him if things went wrong.

CHAPTER XVII

Mrs. Farrar Serves Notice

Sid was whipping cream in the pantry. Her mother had gone downtown to do some shopping and left her to prepare the dessert for dinner. The girl's mind was easier than it had been. She believed that no matter how wild her brother Earl had been, he was not guilty of helping to hold up the First National van. Moreover, she had in a measure shifted the responsibility to broader shoulders. Peter Moran was her friend. He would look after her and see that Earl was given fair play. Somehow she had a great deal of confidence in Peter.

In fact, today, she felt quite gay and happy. David Summers had asked her to go with him to a dance, and she was very, very fond of David. It seemed as though the clouds were breaking and she had a right to be glad she was young and in a good world. So she sang as she worked.

"East is East, West is West,"

her young voice lifted.

She was not afraid even if Murphy and Hall were upstairs and her mother out of the house. As a matter of fact, she never was in fear of Murphy in the same way that she was of Hall. Tim might hold over her head a threat about Earl, but he had in him some spark of manhood that made her feel he would not injure her personally nor permit anybody else to do so. The other man, with his sallow face and furtive eyes, gave her a scunner, as her Scotch grandmother might have said. She felt the shivers run up her back when he looked at her.

"Follow the Swallow back home,"

she sang, and then abruptly stopped both the song and the whipping of the cream.

From upstairs came voices, quick, imperative; and after these heavy, crashing sounds. She paused, the beater in her still fingers snatched into instant apprehension. The noise continued. It was as though the house were being battered to pieces. Whatever could they be doing? Her soft eyes filled with fear. This sudden rending of the silence set her trembling.

Then, while the shock of it still held her tense, there came sharp, menacing reports of a gun. Four times she heard them, and each detonation hit her with an almost physical impact. She had lived a quiet life, one far from scenes of violence, and her competence had not been tested by such situations. A shiver ran down her spine. Her terror was no less because it held the mystery of the unknown as well as the certain knowledge that friend and foe had come to an issue. Very likely someone lay dead in the room above.

Came voices, harsh and threatening, and then again—silence.

Sid waited, how long she did not know, summoning her courage to go up and learn what was wrong, whether her friend was the victim of a murderous attack. She dared not run screaming into the street, for that would bring the police and possibly disaster to her brother.

84

From above there came sounds again—of footsteps, of something heavy being dragged across the floor. She braced herself to go up. She told herself she must go—now—at once. Yet she could not go. It was strange, but her muscles refused to obey her will. They would carry her as far as the foot of the back stairs and no farther. They balked, as though afflicted by some paralysis.

She found herself at last upon the stairs, her fluttering heart heavy with dread. Slowly, step by step, she took the treads, pausing between them to listen for some audible expression of the sinister fact she feared in that room above. At the landing she waited again, calling for the stark pluck to finish what she had begun. Somehow she found it at last and her trembling limbs moved forward.

From Moran's room came voices and rustling sounds. She caught sight of the shattered door, the panels torn to fragments, splintered bits scattered on the hall floor.

Her first reluctant look into the room did not show her what she had dreaded, the picture her startled imagination had flashed to the mind. Upon the floor was no crumpled body. Nor were there signs of anybody having been wounded.

Two men were in the bedroom—Murphy and Hall. The place was a litter of confusion. Drawers had been torn from the chiffonier and their contents emptied upon the floor. Clothes and shoes had been tossed from the closet. The bed had been stripped of its linen and the mattress turned half over. Even the rug had been ripped up and flung into a corner.

Hall was the first to catch sight of the girl. He was at her immediately, snarling and cursing, his hands reaching for her throat.

"You're in this with him. Where is it? What have you done with it?" he cried furiously.

She shrank back from his grasp. His face was appalling in its savagery. "No—no! I don't know what you mean," she told him, trying to push him back with her hands.

"You gave him a key," he shrieked, his fingers fastening on her. "You double-crosser! You—you——"

Murphy tore him away. "Let the girl alone," he ordered. "Keep your hands off her. If she knows anything I'll get it out of her."

The other man showed his teeth. "Where'd you get that stuff? I'll cut her heart out but I'll make her talk."

"Say, fellow, listen!" Murphy towered over him. "You'll leave her alone. See! You'll keep your dirty hands to yourself. I'm tellin' you. Me, Tim Murphy."

To Sidney it seemed for an instant that Hall was going to accept the issue. She could hear the grinding of his teeth as he clenched them. Apparently he thought better of it. He shrugged his shoulders and decided to give way.

"Now, girl, come clean," Murphy ordered.

"I don't know what you mean," she faltered. "What is it you want? Tell me."

"He robbed us—that fellow Moran—got all we had in the room. Did you help him? Where did he get a key to our room? What do you know?"

"Nothing," she pleaded. "I didn't know he was in the house. I didn't. I didn't. I've been downtown."

"You don't know when he got back?"

"No."

"What did he do with it? Where did he put it? We're going to look in your room, girl."

"You may. There's nothing there. It isn't locked. It never is when I'm out."

"Anyhow, you'll go with us while we look." Murphy took her by the arm, not roughly, and pushed her in front of him.

They searched her room, tossing all her belongings hither and yon in their eager quest. What they were looking for was nowhere in be found there.

Hall sidled up to her, his teeth bared. "If you're holdin' back on us, girl, I'll—I'll——"

The vagueness of his threat made it no less alarming. It was the man himself—what he was—that made his words dreadful to her. Sidney shuddered.

"Leave her alone, I tell you," growled Murphy.

Hall turned on him, prudence and patience both exhausted. His hand slid to a pocket. "You can't make that stuff stick with me," he snarled.

They stood glaring at each other, these two men, their eyes charged with fury, their poised tenseness animate with danger.

At that critical moment came an interruption, the sound of a curt crisp voice. "What's this? What's it all about?"

Mrs. Farrar stood in the doorway, a figure of solid and capable resolution. All of them were taken by surprise. Sid drew a deep breath of relief. The menace in the attitude of the men vanished at once and their rage collapsed. They had been put on the defensive. Moreover, they had no explanation to offer. They stood looking at her helplessly.

"What's been going on here?" the landlady demanded. "Tell me before I telephone for the police."

"He robbed us," Murphy replied sulkily.

"Who robbed you?"

"That Moran. He got into our room while we were downtown and robbed us."

"Robbed you of what?"

There was a moment of silence before Murphy answered the question. "Our money."

"Got into your room, you say. How did he do that, if you left it locked?"

"That's what we don't know. But he did—and took a lot of our money."

"Then you'd better call the police. I'll get them on the 'phone."

She was turning to go, but Murphy stopped her. "No, ma'am, don't do that. I reckon it's better not."

"Better not. What do you mean? If any of my boarders claim they have been robbed in my house I want an investigation, one under the proper authorities."

"It would give a bad name to the house," Hall said.

Mrs. Farrar looked straight at him in the disconcerting fashion she had. "I'll risk that, young man." Her mind came to another phase of the matter. "If your money has been stolen, what are you doing in my daughter's room? Are you looking for it here?"

"We thought he might have hidden it here, ma'am."

"What nonsense! I don't understand this at all. I'll just call the police and see what they have to say."

Murphy's jaw tightened. "No, ma'am. That don't suit us. We've got the say about this. It's our money he took. We'll attend to it ourselves."

"You'll not attend to it by tearing my house to pieces," she informed him. At that moment her eyes fell upon the splintered fragments of the door. "Who did that?" she demanded.

"Moran," answered Hall instantly.

"He didn't either," Sid put in indignantly. "They did it themselves, trying to get into his room."

The landlady had stepped up the hall and was examining the damaged entry. "It's broken from the outside. Why should Mr. Moran have done it—when he had his key with him?"

"He didn't have it with him. He claimed he lost it on the way home," Hall told her.

Her direct look held him once more. "Another lie, young man. I was here when he came home and when he went into his room. And he couldn't have locked the door again unless he had the key with him."

Murphy abandoned that fiction as untenable. "No, ma'am, we broke it. He'd stolen our money and was inside. He wouldn't let us in, so we had to break the door."

"You had to break the door of a room in my house?" Mrs. Farrar asked ominously.

"We'll pay for the damage," Murphy promised sullenly.

"You'll do that—and you'll get out—tonight. There's something wrong here. I don't know what it is, but I'll have nothing more to do with any of you. I'm through with you all."

"We'll go tomorrow—not tonight, ma'am," Hall slid in. "The town's full and we can't get a room. Tomorrow ma'am."

"Tonight. There are plenty of rooms at Hilltown. You can go there. I'll not put up with such doings in my house. You'll both go—and he'll go too."

Hall's cold, fishy eyes looked at her insolently. "We'll go when we're good and ready—and you'll not call the police either. An' it won't be tonight we'll go. You've got another guess coming."

"We're not looking for trouble ma'am," Murphy explained to her. "We're willing to go tomorrow, but we want to stay and see if we can't find our money. He lit out so fast we think he left it here somewhere."

Sid spoke to her mother in a low voice. "That's not all. They were shooting up here at Mr. Moran. That's why I came up—when I heard the shots."

"Shooting," her mother repeated. "In my house. That settles it. I'll have the police in right away."

Hall barred the way, grinning evilly at her. "I wouldn't do that if I was you, lady. It would be too bad if you did. Ask her—ask the girl. She'll tell you."

"What do you mean?" Mrs. Farrar turned on her daughter. "What do you know about this, Sid?" she asked sharply.

Sid had tried to spare her mother, but she knew now that her hand was forced. If she did not tell, Hall would. "They say—these men do—that Earl was in with them on the bank robbery." She spoke as though the words were being dragged out of her.

"What bank robbery?"

"The Hilltown First National."

"They mean—that Earl helped them do it?" The mother spoke incredulously. Yet dismay was knocking at the door of her heart.

"Yes. That's what they say—that they did it and Earl helped."

The mother turned on them with swift feminine ferocity. "Did you drag my boy into this with you? If you did—if you dared——"

Hall showed his teeth, as a cornered wolf does. "Forget that line. He went in—that is, if any of us did, which I ain't admitting. But say we pulled the job—all right. He's in it right up to the neck, same as the rest of us an' worse. *See!*"

"Where is he now?"

"We don't know. He lit out. I don't blame him either. You see, ma'am, Earl's the one that croaked the driver."

Mrs. Farrar's heart turned over. She put a hand on the wall to steady herself.

"I don't believe it," she cried. "It's not true. It's a wicked lie."

Hall's broken-toothed smile was cruel as he said, "You'd better believe it. He's the one will swing if we get caught."

The eyes of the mother closed for a moment. She felt curiously faint, she who never had fainted in her life.

Sid came to her aid with comfort and support. She put an arm around her mother. "Don't believe it, Mother. It's not true. Earl left Hilltown the day before the robbery. I've got proof of it. He told me so himself."

"Have you seen him? Is he here?" demanded Hall.

The girl's eyes met his. "No, I haven't seen him, but I've had a letter."

"What did he say? Anything about this express job?"

"Not a word."

"Then how do you know he claims he wasn't in it?"

"Because it was written on the train near Kansas City the day before the robbery."

"Slick work. He wrote it after an' dated it before."

"But he didn't. The postmark was the morning of the eleventh."

89

"Show me the letter."

"She'll do nothing of the kind." Mrs. Farrar's courage had come surging back. Her voice was strong, her manner dominant. She seemed almost to pounce at the men. "Out you get —the pair of you. Now, before dinner tonight. You'll settle for the damage first. It's either that—or the police."

Hall's eyes looked murder. But there was nothing to do but give way. He could hear someone moving about downstairs. The boarders were coming back from their day's work.

"All right. It's your house, and your say-so. What's the damage, Mrs. Farrar? Make it enough. We'll pay what's right." This from Murphy, who realized now that threats would carry them no further.

The landlady named a price. Murphy paid it and settled their bill.

"You want to remember one thing," Hall warned her. "If we go to the pen your son goes too. Bite on that hard."

Fifteen minutes later he and Hall left with their suitcases. Mrs. Farrar was at the door to see them depart.

This done, she drew her daughter into the parlour for a moment. She had been too busy watching the preparations of her departing guests to raise a point which had occurred to her.

"Where's the letter from your brother? And why didn't you show it to me?" she asked.

"I haven't had any letter from him," Sidney told her. "That was just a bluff."

"Then you don't know that he wasn't in Hilltown the day of the robbery?" the mother asked anxiously.

"Yes, I almost knew it before. I'm sure of it now. You saw they didn't call my bluff, as Earl says. If it hadn't been true they would have stood out against me. But they didn't. They practically admitted it. Besides, I've heard Earl left—or, at least, one of their crowd, and by the description it must have been him. The police at Hilltown found it out and Mr. Moran told me."

"Who is this Moran? What's he got to do with it? Sit down, child, and tell me all you know."

She did.

Her mother listened, and as mothers will till the end of time wept over her erring son. Later no doubt she prayed for him, remembering him when he had been a fat and cuddly little baby crowing in her arms and she had been a proud young wife rejoicing in her firstborn.

CHAPTER XVIII

Tightening the Net

Peter and Jim, after the latter had done some telephoning, slipped quietly from the rooming-house and made their way downtown. It was still raining, but only with a faint drizzle. Clouds were scudding across the sky, and there was the promise of a break in its gloom, perhaps even of a coming moon.

The two men did not go by main, lighted streets but kept as much as they could to darker and less travelled ones. They were not anxious to be recognized, and they were not the only ones in that state of mind. On the other side of the street two men passed carrying suitcases. It was too dark to recognize faces at that distance. Otherwise there would have been trouble instantly; for the two with the suitcases were Murphy and Hall.

At the City Hall, Peter and his friend turned into the lower floor, where the police headquarters were located. They asked the desk sergeant for the Chief, and as soon as they gave their names were admitted to his private office. A group of people were gathered there, including Carey and his daughter, Burlson, three of the detective's men, and the Chief of Police of Petrolia.

Peter looked his surprise at sight of Janet.

"I made Dad bring me," she explained. "I could not sit down and wait at home."

"Anything to report, Peter?" asked Carey.

"Yes, sir. Have you explained the situation to the Chief here?" Peter wanted to know.

"Yes. He wants us to co-operate with him in pulling off these arrests. His idea is to swear us all in as special deputies."

"Good! Do you want me to make my report now, sir?"

"Yes. We'll have to get busy at once."

"Hall and Murphy were at the boarding-house when I left. But they are getting restless, sir. I don't think they will stay much longer. It wouldn't surprise me if they left tonight. They are worried, I think."

"What makes you think so?" Burlson asked in his official manner, always touched with pomposity.

Peter gave an expurgated version of his burglary of their room. He omitted to mention that he had found any of the money, but he took from his pocket-book the receipt for the house-rent at Hilltown and handed it to Carey.

Burlson's reproof was sharp and positive. "You had no business going into their room. It was a fool business. Of course they'll light out of town. Probably we've lost them just through your fool interference. I suppose you wanted to get all the credit yourself."

There was a certain justice in the detective's viewpoint. It would have been better to have waited. Of course his fatal error had been in carrying off the money with him. This he had not divulged, and now he was glad of it. Burlson had enough to reproach him with.

Ways and means were discussed. The Chief wanted to make the arrests at once. "If they are ready to be on the wing, we should get them before they fly," he said. "These birds don't linger when they've once made up their mind that a climate is too hot for them."

The detective was of a different opinion. "Let's shadow them and make all the arrests together. Hall and Murphy will join the others this evening to talk the thing over. Perhaps they are doing it right now. We mustn't wait another minute."

This did not suit the Petrolia Chief exactly. He wanted the arrests made in his town and under his orders. There would be a lot of glory in capturing even two of the bandits after the Hilltown police had fallen down on the job. The thing would be a tremendous feather in his cap and would be played up by the newspapers all over the country.

"Better half a loaf than no bread, Mr. Carey, and when we get two, one of them will probably squawk on the others," he argued. "If we wait they'll likely all slip through our fingers."

It was decided to shadow Hall and Murphy for an hour or two, and if they joined their fellows make the arrests then, but in any case not to wait more than two hours.

Burlson and his men left, Dunn going along to show them the house. Peter lingered for a word of further conference with the banker. As soon as he was alone with the Careys he gave them further information.

"There are one or two things I have not told yet, Mr. Carey. The most important is that when I was in their room I found a lot of the stolen money, both bills and silver. The bills were under the rug, the silver in some old shoes. When I heard those fellows coming I dumped the whole thing into a bag that was in the closet and took it to my room."

"You took the bag away with you when you left?"

"No. I had to make sure of it, and there was a chance that I wouldn't leave. They were already hammering at the door of my room. So I dropped the grip from my window into a rain-water barrel below. As I said before I slid down the wistaria vine and dodged around the corner of the house while Hall was shooting at me. The money must be in the rain barrel now."

"Unless they saw you drop it."

"They couldn't have seen me. They were already trying to break in the door."

"Let's go and see if it's in the barrel, though of course it is," Janet proposed eagerly.

"You'll do nothing of the kind, young woman. You're going back to the hotel, and you'll stay there until I call you. Understand?"

Janet understood perfectly. From long experience she could tell when there was any use trying to get her father to change his mind. Now she knew it was as fixed as the Rock of Gibraltar. But as a matter of principle she made one protest.

"Have a heart, Dad. I want to be in on some of the fun."

"I'm going to use my good judgment, Janet, even if you won't use yours," he told her. "There's likely to be trouble. It's more than a likelihood if we meet those fellows."

"Will it be any better for you to get shot than for me, Dad?" she asked. "What am I to tell Mother if anything happens to you?" Janet was distinctly annoyed at the waiting part assigned her.

"Nothing is going to happen to me. I'll recall to your mind a promise you made before you left Hilltown, that you would do exactly as I told you. I expect you to keep that promise. If you don't want to I'll have to send you back home."

Janet surrendered, apparently. "All right. But hurry, please. Then you can catch up with Mr. Burlson and his men. There won't be any danger if you are all together. And do come back as soon as you can, Dad. You, too, Peter."

Peter and Carey left Janet at the hotel and followed the

officers to the boarding-house. They went to the front of the house.

"We can't go sneaking up to the back by the alley-way," Peter said. "Either our friends or our enemies might pot away at us. I don't suppose it's any pleasanter to be shot by mistake than on purpose."

They were on the pavement on the opposite side of the street from the Farrar home. Peter caught Carey's arm and gave it a slight pressure. "Somebody is standing there—in the shadow of the big tree."

Carey nodded. "Yes, I see him. Probably one of our detectives. Shall I call to him?"

"No, let me go forward and make sure."

Peter walked forward, as a chance passer might, but his hand was on the butt of his revolver.

The waiting man was Burlson. Peter signalled Carey to come forward.

"No sign of our birds yet," the detective said. "Wonder if you've scared 'em away. I'll bet you have."

"Likely enough," Peter assented. "Why not send one of your men to the door to find out? He could ask Mrs. Farrar. If Hall and Murphy are there he could take a message to them that Tige and Lynch wanted to see them."

"Sure. That they wanted them to come to where they're staying. Not a bad notion. Then we can trail these birds there and bag the whole outfit. I'll do that. I'll have Mike go to the door."

Burlson vanished in the darkness. It was nearly ten minutes later when he returned. He was visibly put out.

"They've gone, bag and baggage. Mrs. Farrar doesn't know where and she says she doesn't care. Says she's through with 'em for good and all. Mike says she was mighty cool to him. I reckon she thought Mike was a friend of theirs." He went on, speaking to Peter: "You see now what you've done. We had run down these birds—had 'em sewed up in a sack—and you butt in an' ruin the whole play."

"Yes, it was a foolish business," admitted Peter. "But hadn't we better be heading them off from making a get-away?"

"I was coming to that," Burlson said peevishly. "I've sent the boys to report to the Chief. I'm going along now to advise him about closing all the roads and 'phoning to the towns roundabout. They'll probably make a break for Hilltown, but you never can tell."

"The trains and inter-urban cars ought to be watched," Carey suggested.

"I'll attend to all that," Burlson told him. "I'm gonna 'phone myself to the Chief at Hilltown to have all the points watched where they could get in either by a motor or in trains. You better come along with me, Mr. Carey. But I'm leaving this young fellow and his friend Dunn to watch the house. They can't do any more mischief now."

"I'll be along in a few minutes, Burlson," the banker told him. "I have something to talk over with Peter first. Don't wait for me."

"It's not likely they'll come back," Burlson said as he left. "No reason why they should. But there's just a chance. They might have left something."

"That's so. They might," agreed Peter, and in the darkness the detective did not see the twinkle in his eyes.

"You can't always tell about crooks. They do queer things. Now, if they're soft on this girl, either one or both of 'em why, they might stop as they left town to date up with her or something. No one can tell. If it wasn't for the woman in the case we'd sometimes have poor luck running down criminals. But they're always liable to lose their heads over their women."

"Miss Farrar isn't their woman. She's a sweet, shy girl. I thought I had made that clear," Peter said.

"That's all right. I'm not saying she is and I'm not saying she isn't. One thing this business teaches a man is that a woman involved in a case never tells the truth where her man is concerned."

Burlson bustled away importantly.

Carey smiled. "He likes to feel he's running the affair. That's why he is elated at having a chance to take you down a peg, Peter. Your work was a reflection on his. You were getting along too fast. Naturally he's pleased because you made a mistake."

"I certainly made one," Peter admitted ruefully. "Afraid I've spilled the beans. A fool business. I agree with Burlson on that. But there's one thing. Hall and Murphy are more likely to return than he thinks, since he doesn't know that I copped a large share of their loot. They'll not give it up without

95

trying to get it back. They know I didn't take it with me, so it must be on the premises. That's how they'll reason. It wouldn't surprise me if all four of them returned and made a thorough search of the house and premises. They've got beyond caution now. They might hold up the house and its occupants while they made their search."

Dunn had joined them. They walked around to the back of the house.

CHAPTER XIX

The Safety Deposit Box

"Our safety deposit vault is at this corner," Peter explained. "That's the window of my room. I came down hanging on to the wistaria vine while Hall was firing at me."

Peter had brought with him an electric flashlight. He turned it on the barrel, with a little gesture of introduction, "Gentlemen, our private box."

Gesture and voice both fell to anti-climax. Peter stared, unwilling to believe his eyes. The rain barrel held no water—and no brown bag.

"Gone," he said. "They've beaten us to it."

Carey peered over his shoulder into the empty barrel. "They must have seen you drop the bag."

"Yes," acquiesced Peter. "But how could they? They were battering at my hall door, and it was dark."

"Perhaps someone else saw you," the banker suggested.

"Maybe. Or they found it later."

Dunn borrowed the torch and examined the barrel. He looked up, an odd expresion on his face.

"You put the money here?" he asked.

"I dropped it from the window just before I swung out— dropped it into the barrel, which was full of water."

"And they shot at you while you were coming down. Is that the way it was?"

"Yes."

"From that window over to the right. I reckon?"

"Yes."

"Hmp! They shot away the lock of yore safety deposit box."

"What do you mean?"

"Looky here!"

The cow-puncher turned the light of the torch on a little round hole low down in one of the barrel staves. "See! One of the bullets tore in here. It musta gone out at the bottom." He shifted the light, sweeping it to and fro across the bottom. "Sure. Here's the place. Two good bung-holes pung through the wood to let the water out. Consequence is yore barrel emptied. Now it's quit rainin' no more is fallin' in."

Peter nodded. "I suppose they tried to follow me and found the bag in the empty barrel."

"Looks that-away," Dunn agreed. "You had a darned good idea when you dropped the grip here, but the luck wasn't breakin' yore way. It's a cinch they won't come back now. There's nothin' for them to come back for. I'm guessin' that they're hot-footin' it for Hilltown or the northern state line right now. An' they've sure got the laugh on us."

"Yes, that must be the way of it," agreed Carey. "Our only hope now is that Burlson and the police have blocked the roads and will catch them while they are trying to escape. We may lose them all, thanks to my darned foolishness."

"Or we may lose them all, thanks to my darned foolishness," Peter said. "More likely it will be that way. It's easier to catch your birds before they fly the coop than after. I've done the very thing I was afraid the police would do, bungled the job by scaring them away."

"Well it can't be helped," Carey said by way of consolation. "We all make mistakes now and then. I think we'll drop in and have a little chat with Mrs. Farrar. She may be able to tell us something. There's just a chance she found the bag."

Carey had another reason too for wanting to see that lady. He had considerable respect for Peter's judgment, but he thought he would like to see the landlady and her daughter with his own eyes. They might be in this robbery to the extent of knowing more than Peter thought they did.

Mrs. Farrar did not receive them with any enthusiasm. As she opened the door and barred the entrance her mouth set grimly.

"I've brought Mr. Carey with me to have a little talk with you, Mrs. Farrar," explained Peter. "Mr. Carey is the president of——"

The landlady cut him off curtly. "I don't want to talk with him or you or anybody else. I've had quite enough of all of you, Mr. Moran. If you'll get your things out of my house to-night I'll be obliged to you."

Carey took up the task of appeasing her. "You have plenty of cause for complaint, Mrs. Farrar. But Peter is not to blame. The fact is that you have unfortunately been imposed upon by a gang of desperate criminals."

"It seems so," she cut in acidly. "I ought to know it, since my house has been torn to pieces and turned into a shooting gallery."

"Which nobody regrets more than I do, Mrs. Farrar," the banker went on. "I am James Carey of the First National at Hilltown. These men who lodged with you undoubtedly were the ones who robbed the bank. We're trying to clear up this matter, and I feel sure that then you'll be put to no more inconveniences."

"I certainly hope so," she said uncompromisingly, holding the door ready to close.

"We have a few questions we would like to ask, if you don't mind."

"I'm busy, and I don't intend to get mixed up in this thing," she said decisively.

"Of course not, so you'll welcome the chance to clear it up. If we can step into the parlour——"

"No, thank you. I prefer not to talk."

Carey's voice hardened a little. "Perhaps I ought to tell you that we are officers of the law. It would be much better for you to talk with us and tell us anything you may know. Of course we can enter without your permission. That is not the question."

"Then what is the question?" she asked bluntly.

"Whether you are or are not giving aid and support to criminals wanted by the law," he retorted sharply.

She stood hesitating for a moment, then "Come in!" she said, and stood aside to let them pass.

They filed into the sitting-room. Peter stepped at once to the windows and drew the blinds carefully. He did not care to be interrupted by a shot from the darkness outside. Mrs. Farrar offered chairs rigidly. They seated themselves. She remained standing.

Carey broke the silence. "Do you know anything about these men—who they are, where they came from, where they used to live before they came here?"

"No."

98

There were folding doors between the front and back parlours. These were open. Through them came a girl shyly. It was Sidney. She stood beside her mother, a hand tucked under the elbow of the older woman.

"This is your daughter, I suppose," Carey continued. "Perhaps you can tell us something of them, Miss Farrar."

"No, sir. Mr. Moran used to go to school with that Murphy. Maybe he can tell you."

"You didn't pick up any letters they left, or ever notice any postmarks on letters that came."

"No letters ever came," the girl answered. "They may have got mail when they went down to Hilltown."

"Didn't they in their talk ever tell about places they had been?"

"No-o, except that that Murphy told about being in France during the war. I think the other one spoke about New York once or twice."

Carey turned to the mother. "And you, Mrs. Farrar, you heard nothing that would lead you to guess their antecedents?"

"No." Her monosyllable was defensive, hostile even. It conveyed an intention to tell as little as possible. Peter guessed that she was watching warily, intent on making no admissions that might tell against her family. He wondered if she knew that Earl was under suspicion. Her manner suggested that she did.

The banker put some of his cards on the table. He spoke clearly and decisively, a ring of authority in his voice. "Let us understand each other, Mrs. Farrar. We know a good deal about this thing. We have wound a net about these men from which they cannot escape if they are captured. Among other things we know your son was very friendly to them, or perhaps I should say with them, indeed far too much so for his own good. They are a bad lot."

She seemed to hold herself a little more rigidly, as though she realized on what dangerous ground she stood. "I don't know anything about that," she said, and closed her lips tightly.

"You know he brought them here, that he went to Hilltown with them, that he stayed in the house they rented there. You know that, don't you?" Carey flung back sharply.

"He didn't bring them here. They came, and I took them as I might any other boarders."

"I ought to warn you that you are not doing your son's cause any good by this attitude," the banker said. "If you protect these men we have a right to assume you have a reason for it."

"Mother," implored the girl in a low voice.

"Just a moment, Mrs. Farrar," Peter interrupted. "We know Earl is only a boy, and we know he wasn't actually in this job. He left Hilltown for Kansas City the day before the robbery. Perhaps he knew about it and was afraid to tell. Anyhow, he left early in the morning, secretly, so that he would not be seen by them. It may easily be that he dared not tell what he knew or guessed, and that flight seemed to him the only way out. In any case he is young and was not present at the hold-up. We want to stand between him and trouble if we can. Certainly I do, and I think Mr. Carey is with me in that. We can use him as a witness against the others if we find him. What we want you to understand is that we are not enemies to your son but far more his friends than are those scoundrels who tried to lead him astray. Is that not true, Mr. Carey?"

"Precisely," assented the banker. "I am willing—more than willing—to try to protect him if I can. But it will be difficult to do this if Mrs. Farrar persists in assuming that we are enemies, and if she refuses to co-operate with us."

A muscle twitched in the face of the harassed mother, but after a moment's reflection she surrendered. "I'll tell anything I know," she said.

"Good! said Carey. "You'll find we can be trusted to keep our words. We'll stand by the boy if you and your daughter and the boy himself permit us to do so by helping us run to earth this gang of murderous criminals."

"What do you want me to tell you?"

"Do you know where your son is? Have you had any communication from him whatever in any way?"

"No, sir." Peter thought the words came after a moment's hesitation. Her eyes were anxious, almost fearful.

"If you do please let us know at once. We want him as a witness and to find out what he knows about these fellows."

"I'll let you know at once." The woman's hands trembled slightly. She was far from wholly reassured. Some secret was on her mind.

After two or three more questions in regard to the habits

of the men and their acquaintances, Carey abruptly shot another query at her.

"Do you know, Mrs. Farrar, or you, Miss Farrar, that these men shot a hole in the rain-water barrel back of the house?"

The surprised and puzzled look on the faces of the women appeared a sufficient answer. It was as though each one asked herself why, even if this were true, he should refer to it at this time. Mrs. Farrar shook her head.

"I didn't know it—no. Sidney said they were shooting before I returned from town."

"And you, Miss Farrar?"

"No." The girl could not understand why he asked. It seemed trivial.

"Have either of you seen anything during the past two hours of a bag, a grip for hand baggage, made of brown imitation alligator hide?"

"No," Sidney replied. "But that Hall had a bag like that. I've seen it in his room when I was sweeping. Probably he took it with him.

"But he didn't," volunteered Mrs. Farrar. "I watched them pack and stayed with them till they left. They didn't have such a bag with them."

Peter leaned forward in his chair, forearm on knee. "Quite sure, Mrs. Farrar? This is rather important."

"Yes. I was at the door just behind them when they left. If they had had it, I would have seen it."

"Why were you watching them so closely?" asked Carey.

"To make sure they didn't take anything that didn't belong to them. I didn't trust them. When I ordered them out of the house they didn't want to go, so I followed them up pretty closely. They had been ransacking different rooms, and I didn't intend they should any more."

"Did they go down the walk to the street or did they turn back into the garden first?"

"They went right down the street. I stood on the porch and watched them go."

"Have either you or your daughter been in the back yard since that time?" said Carey.

Each of the women said that she had not.

"Do you know anybody else in the house that has been?"

"No, sir. What would they go dragging through the wet grass and bushes for in this rain?" Mrs. Farrar replied.

There were more questions, more answers, but these developed chiefly the facts that were already known to Carey and Peter.

As they were leaving, Sidney turned to Peter eagerly and anxiously. "You won't forget, Mr. Moran, will you—about being a friend to Earl?"

"No, we'll not forget. This may be the best thing that could have happened to him. It will bring him up short with a jerk. If he escapes the law—and I feel sure he will if he plays fair with us—he's not likely to slip into another intimacy with men of this stamp. Don't worry about him. I think he'll be all right."

The girl choked down a sob. "Oh, I do hope so. He's really a good boy. If you only knew—— But he does get wild and restless."

Carey patted her head in a kindly way. He had a girl of his own and felt tender toward this one who had such a helpless childish look in her soft eyes.

"It's going to be all right, I think. Anyhow, we'll do all we can for him."

"Oh, thank you—thank you, sir!" she murmured.

CHAPTER XX

Peter Bumps into Action

Outside the three men stopped for a moment's consultation. The rain had ceased, and at intervals the moon showed from behind scudding clouds.

"I don't understand this thing," Peter said. "Either they did not find the brown bag or else they emptied its contents into another suitcase before they left. If they did that last, either they left the brown bag in their room or they threw it away somewhere. The only place they could throw it handily would be out of the window into the garden shrubbery. Think I'll run back there for a moment and have a look. Wait for me across the street, please, will you?"

"Dunn might run upstairs and have a look in their room," Carey suggested.

"Why not? While I'm looking in the back yard. And you

wait for us, Mr. Carey?" Peter stopped to call over his shoulder, "I'll be back as soon as you are, Jim."

Peter ran around the house, turned a corner—and bumped hard into the figure of a man. For an instant the two glared at each other, then simultaneously both swung into action.

A fist crashed into Peter's face as his arms closed on the body of the man into whom he had run. The man was the one whom Sidney had called Tige, the one who had trailed him to Hilltown earlier in the day.

The man lifted up his voice in a low guarded shout. "It's that Moran. Gun him, Jake."

The two locked in each other's arms were too close for the use of firearms. Neither dared let loose of the other long enough to reach for a gun. They swayed as they struggled, muscles hardening as they came into play. Instinctively Peter swung round in such a way as to put his foe's body between himself and the third man running forward. He raised his own voice in a shout for help, nor did he soft-pedal the sound of it as Tige had done. For he did not need to worry lest some officer of the law hear him.

Never in his gusty lifetime had Peter needed help more. The light of the racing moon flashed on steel and Peter crouched low behind the bulwark of his antagonist's body. A gun roared into his ears. He and Tige, still thrashing around, crashed into the water barrel and went down, still locked closely together. As he fell, Peter caught a glimpse of the other man dodging about them in the attempt to get in a second shot without running the risk of hitting the flying legs or whirling body of his partner.

Peter fell on top of his opponent, but with one strong heave rolled over bringing the body of the other above his own. For the present he preferred to be underneath. In that position less of his body was exposed to the fire of the second bandit.

He knew it was a question of seconds. At any moment a gun might be thrust against his body; at any moment he might feel the impact of a bullet tearing through his vitals. But none came.

A deep shout lifted to high heaven. Looking up, Peter saw a figure balanced on the window-sill of his room. In the light of a fugitive moon it looked huge as it came hurtling down. An instant later the outlaw with the revolver went to earth as

103

though he had been poleaxed. One hundred and seventy-five pounds of cow-puncher had landed on his shoulders.

There was a moment of breathless silence, then the sound of feeble struggling and a heavy fist beating upon flesh.

An urgent distressed voice called. "Help, Tige, help! He's killin' me."

Tige was in no position to help. Reassured as to his second enemy, Peter whirled suddenly, using the barrel staves as a lever for his foot to help him turn. He and his opponent rolled over and over, grappling for better holds. When they brought up against the wall, Peter was for the moment on top.

He braced his feet and pinned the other's arms to the side of his body. Tige fought desperately to break the hold, and Peter realized with a sinking heart that it would be a matter of moments until he did; for his own strength was going. He had not in him the reserves of force that had been his before he had been shot at the hold-up.

Hanging on to hold his advantage, Peter's head was buried in the other man's shoulder. He felt a sudden relaxation of Tige's muscles, and at the same instant a voice came to him.

"Don't struggle or I'll blow a hole through your head."

It was Carey's voice, cold, hard, merciless.

The writhing frame of the outlaw collapsed.

Carey had arrived in time, and just in time. Peter got up and leaned weakly against the wall. His breath came raggedly from his heaving chest.

The battle was over. Dunn's opponent, never for a moment with a chance to win, surrendered at discretion. He could no longer endure Jim's pile-driving fists.

"I quit. I give up," he said huskily. "Lay off me before you've killed me."

The cow-puncher pinned the fellow's two wrists beneath one of his hands and with the other searched his clothes for a second gun. The first had gone flying when Jim's weight bore him to earth. Jim rose, picked up the weapon, and dropped it into his pocket.

"Lie right there, fellow, with yore arms stretched out till I give the word. An' don't you make any mistake. See!" To the banker he said, "If you'll look after this guy, Mr. Carey, I'll frisk the other one. If he wriggles a finger, plug him. Don't take any chances."

Jim devoted his attention to Tige. "Fellow, don't you make

any breaks either. This gun in my hand goes off mighty easy. First off, roll over on yore face. That'll do. If you've got a gun I want it. Good. Now I've drawn yore teeth so's you can't bite you may get up an' stand against the wall with yore hands reachin' for the sky. Yes, that-away. You other fellow step along here too. Watch him, Mr. Carey."

"What'll we do with them?" asked Carey.

"Take 'em into the house an' 'phone for the police, I'd say." Jim suggested.

"I don't think so," Peter disagreed. "We'd better get them to Hilltown if we can. The jail here is none too strong. Their pals might pull off a jail delivery by bribing the jailer. That would not be possible at Hilltown. Why not take them to the garage where your car is and drive back to Hilltown where we can see them put securely under lock and key?"

"The Chief of Police here wouldn't stand for that if he knew," Carey said doubtfully.

"He doesn't need to know till after it is over. You can get your car past the guards of course."

"We-ell," agreed Carey doubtfully, "perhaps it would be better."

Once more they knocked at the door of the house and were admitted by Mrs. Farrar. She identified the two men at once as the ones whom she had seen frequently with Hall and Murphy.

"I heard a shot," she said, and her statement was a question.

Peter nodded toward the stout little bandit. "Mr. Lynch was responsible for it. The bullet was meant for me, but he didn't shoot straight. We want to get a piece of your clothes-line, Mrs. Farrar, to tie up these men."

Lynch was patting his bruised face with a handkerchief Peter had taken from the man's pocket. He pitied himself very much. He had never before met so violently such a hard and knotted fist as the one which very recently had played a tattoo upon his soft, fat face. He glared at Peter resentfully.

"You got no right to hold us. We're not gonna stand for any such raw deal."

"That can easily be explained to the police," Peter said. "If they think they have nothing against you, why, of course they'll let you go."

Mrs. Farrar brought the clothes-line and Dunn tied the hands of the men securely behind their backs.

"It would be better to bring the car here than to take these men through the streets to the garage," Carey said. "Peter, will you go to the hotel and get Janet, then have her order the car and bring it here?"

"Yes, sir. I suggest that the front and back doors be locked and not opened until we get back. It won't be long. There may be an attempt at rescuing them. If their friends miss them and get anxious—why, we don't know what they will do."

"Good enough. We'll be careful. Look out for yourself when you step out, Peter."

Peter did, very carefully. The road seemed to be clear, so he stepped out. But every foot of the way down the dark street he felt nervous. It was impossible for him to keep from quickening his pace, though he did not actually break into a run. Presently he turned into a better-lighted street which led to Petrolia's leading hotel.

The lobby was full of people, as it always was nowadays, talking and smoking in little groups and moving to and fro, going and coming. Peter went to the desk and asked to be connected with the room of Miss Carey.

As he did so Janet came forward and asked for her key.

"I was looking for you," he said. "Your father sent me to get you. He wants us to get the car from the garage and join him at Mrs. Farrar's."

CHAPTER XXI

Carey is Annoyed

"Anything new?" Janet asked in a low voice.

Peter noticed that her bright eyes were gleaming with excitement. This surprised him a little, though he did not know why it should.

"We've got two of 'em," he answered, in a murmur as low as her own. "What garage is the car at?"

"Two of them. Tell me," her whisper cried.

"We found them at the house. Your father and Dunn captured them. We want to get them out of town before the news spreads. So I was sent to get you and the car."

"The car is at the door now. I thought it better to have it handy in case it was wanted."

"Thoughtful of you," he nodded.

"Yes, wasn't it? Since Dad has voted me out of all the fun I can at least be useful, can't I?" He sensed a touch of ironic derision in her voice.

They walked out of the side door of the hotel and stepped into the car waiting there.

"It's all right about these men you've arrested, isn't it?" she asked, after Peter had given the chauffeur directions. "None of you were hurt?"

"No," Peter said. "We're all right."

"I knew there would be no danger in going after the bag. Dad's so ridiculous. By the way, I suppose you got it?"

Peter answered her casual question ruefully. "No, we didn't. They must have beat us to it. By bad luck Hall shot a hole in the barrel and the water ran out. Someone found the bag. I suppose they did. And yet—I don't see what these fellows came back for if they got the bag."

"Too bad," she said sympathetically.

They were moving down the street and Peter lifted the tube to give further directions to the driver. The man nodded his head, a little impatiently, and wheeled into a side street.

"Carter came from this town. He lived here practically all his life before he came to Hilltown. Probably he knows where Mrs. Farrar lives," Janet explained.

Apparently he did, for he stopped in front of the house before Peter knew they had arrived.

Three honks brought Carey and Dunn, with their prisoners, out of the house.

Carey gave directions as to the seating. He himself got in beside Janet in the rear seat. The prisoners took the two jumper seats in front. Peter sat on the other side of Janet and Dunn outside beside the chauffeur.

"I've searched the back yard," the cow-puncher explained. "The bag's not there, and it's not in the yard of the next house as far as I can make out."

At the outskirts of Petrolia the car was stopped by police officers, but when Carey let them know who he was the driver was permitted to continue. They roared through the night over the wet concrete for five level miles. Then the paved road ended and they began to climb hills and swing around

107

curves. On the way to Hilltown they passed a dozen cars, Carter going by them with the expert accuracy of the young trained driver. As they came into Hilltown the car was stopped again.

"Looks as though the police were on the job," Peter said to Janet while Carey talked with the officers outside.

So far as these patrolmen knew, the other bandits had not been arrested yet. There had been no sign of them on the Petrolia-Hilltown road.

Carey brought his head back into the car. "There's a police auto about a mile down the road. We'll turn over our prisoners to the officers in it," he said. Then, "Ouch, what's this darned thing I've been bumping my foot on?" he demanded of Janet.

"I put it there," she told him with feminine calmness. "Am I supposed never to have any baggage? When I want it moved I'll let you know, Dad."

The two prisoners were delivered to the police at the stipulated place. Dunn went along with the three officers in order to report later to Carey what the result of the search of their persons might disclose. Peter was about to go too, but Janet stopped him.

"I want you to go home with us, Peter," she told him. "You can go down to the police station later if you like."

The chauffeur presently drew up at the Carey house. Peter descended and helped Janet out. Mr. Carey followed. They were starting for the house when Janet said casually to Peter, "You might bring my bags along if you like."

Peter dived back into the car and found two bags. The smaller one was quite heavy. He trudged up the walk after the Careys and followed them into the living-room. Mrs. Carey, they gathered from a maid, was out at a reception being given for a visiting English novelist.

"Put the brown bag on the table, Peter," ordered Janet.

He did so, and started at it with bulging eyes. It was not only a brown bag; it was made of imitation alligator skin; moreover, it had the soggy appearance of having recently been in a flood.

"What's that?" demanded Carey sharply.

Janet smiled demurely but maliciously as she said, "That? Oh, that's the old bag you were making so much fuss about letting me help you get."

"How did you come by it?"

"Oh, I fished it out of a rain-water barrel," she told him with *insouciance*.

"When?" her father asked in astonishment.

"I expect it was just before you went to look for it. I met Carter in the car as you left. So I had him run me out to the alley back of Mrs. Farrar's. He knows the house well. That was all there was to it. I walked in the back gate, lifted this out of the barrel, stepped into the car, and said, 'Back to the hotel, Carter.' Very simple, you see."

"I see," her father answered quietly, his eyes stern. "I'll tell you later what I think of the proceeding, young woman."

"If I were younger you'd send me to my room and feed me on bread and water, wouldn't you?" She looked straight at him. Though she was a little afraid, she did not intend to let him know. "Don't you think you were just a little bit arbitrary with me when you cut me out of all the fun, Dad? I thought so. That's why it came over me all of a sudden to slip out and beat you to it with the car."

"And what if these men, the bandits, had been there?"

"I knew they wouldn't be."

"You didn't know anything of the sort," her father told her bluntly. "In point of fact they were there—the two of them we arrested—a very few minutes after you. It was a very foolish thing to do. I'm surprised at you, Janet."

"If you'd let me go with you, it would have been all right. I would have been protected and I'd have got my thrill just the same."

"Yes, you'd have got your thrill. There was a fight. One of these men shot at Peter. Someone might easily have been killed. What business had you there?"

She turned big eyes on Peter. "Did one of them shoot at you?"

"He didn't hit me, anyhow."

"You're always in the thick of it, aren't you?"

"And wishing I weren't," he smiled.

"Old 'Fraid Cat," she teased with a friendly derision that mocked his modesty.

Peter could not help grinning at the impishness of her. It reminded him of a little red-haired girl with pigtails he had once known.

Carey caught his smile and tried to be severe. An attempt was about as far as he could go in matters pertaining to Janet.

"Don't laugh at her," he said. "She doesn't need any encouragement. It was all very well when she was a little girl, but she's grown up now. She ought to know how to behave. A young woman has to be circumspect. She can't do just whatever she takes a fancy to."

"Good gracious, Dad! What an old scold you are." She made a little grimace at him, intended to convey the fact that she was ready to be forgiven.

"Well, anyhow, we might as well see what's in the bag," Carey said.

He pulled down the blinds and closed the door.

"Since Miss Carey found the bag we might let her open it," Peter suggested.

"Janet," she corrected.

"Janet," the young man repeated.

"I've a good mind to send her to her room and not let her see what's in it," her father grumbled.

"I'd steal it again, Dad," she threatened gaily, and she moved forward to the table.

The two men came closer.

"Everybody set?" she asked.

Her father nodded. "Let's see how much is in it?"

She pushed the catch and swung wide the hinge. A very curious and puzzled look came over her face. She stared mutely down at the contents of the bag. She was looking at four nice new vitrified bricks.

CHAPTER XXII

Jack Meredith Shrugs His Shoulders

The three of them stared down at those bricks in sheer astonishment. Janet was the first to find her voice.

"Sold!" she said.

"Where's it gone?" Carey asked. The swiftness of these surprises was rather stunning to logical thought.

"Who took it? And when?" Peter contributed.

"They must have gone to the barrel and got the money, then put the bricks in the bag to fool us," Janet hazarded.

"The bricks came from next door," Peter explained. "They're building a chimeney with them."

"But why—why should these fellows be prowling about if they already had found the money? It's not reasonable." Carey said.

"Unless these two came back to shoot Peter."

"No. They would not do that. Pleasure would have to wait on business, and it was rather urgent for them to be clearing out." This from Peter.

"We can discard that hypothesis," Carey said, exasperated. "But for the life of me I don't see what they were hanging about for."

"Unless someone else got the money," suggested Janet.

"Who, for choice?"

"I don't know. All I know is that I didn't." She could not help laughing a little. "And I thought I was so clever. It serves me right."

"Well, all I've got to say is that I hope there won't be more of these damned surprises," Carey announced with visible irritation. "As you say, in your abominable slang, Janet, I'm about fed-up with them."

"I don't like this last one myself, Dad. I wish I could understand it. But of course we can't. It might be anyone."

"That's the deuce of it," agreed Peter ruefully. "It might be someone who hasn't had a thing to do with this affair—someone who just happened to blunder in. And if so, very likely we'll never be any the wiser."

"Of course there are Mrs. Farrar and her daughter," the banker said reflectively.

"I can't think they did it," Peter replied. "When you shot your question at them about the bag, they both looked completely surprised, as though they couldn't understand why you should be asking such a thing."

"Yes, but that might be camouflage."

"It might, but I don't think so."

The banker was wondering about another angle of the affair. Was it possible that Peter himself had hidden the money and put the bag in the barrel with the bricks in it? He might have done this, knowing that it would come out that he had recovered part of the stolen money. Yet Carey would not believe it. He dismissed the suspicion from his mind.

"Well, *I'm* up a tree," Janet admitted.

"Could someone have put these bricks in after you recovered the bag?" Peter asked her, "Did you leave it alone with the chauffeur?

"Only for a minute while I ran into the hotel. You see, I stayed in the car with it after I got back with the bag. I thought you and Dad would be along soon and I did not want to take it through the hotel lobby, not knowing who might be watching."

"Carter could not have made the transfer. The bricks came, you say, from building going on next door to the boarding-house. It must have been done there," Carey volunteered.

The telephone bell rang. Janet stepped to the receiver.

"Yes. . . . Yes, Jack. We just got back from Petrolia. . . . Heaps of excitement. Why don't you run around here for a minute?"

She hung up. "Jack," she explained. "He's going to drop around. Be here in a minute."

A moment later the bell rang again. This time it was Jim Dunn at the other end of the telephone. He asked for Peter and Janet turned the receiver over to him.

Peter listened, then said to him, "Hold the 'phone a moment, Jim." He turned to Carey. "Jim says the two prisoners have been searched. The police found a lot of bills sewed in their clothing. The amount hasn't been counted yet."

"Good!" said Carey. "That's something, anyhow."

Presently Jack Meredith arrived. Janet had "ditched" a date with him to go to Petrolia. Wherefore he wanted an explanation. Under the circumstances it did not greatly please him to see Peter on the scene.

"What was this hurry-up call to Petrolia?" he asked, a little sulkily. "Thought we had a date at the Forrests' Country Club dance."

"Sorry, Jack. But I couldn't pass up Petrolia," Janet explained. "We've been on a treasure-hunt and sleuthing after criminals and everything. Look what we found."

She led him mysteriously to the table, and after an impressive delay opened the brown bag triumphantly. He looked into it, puzzled.

"Well, what of it?" he asked.

Her laughter rippled out. "It's one on me, Jack. Listen, my child, and I'll tell you the story of the midnight ride of Janet Carey."

She told it, and the rest of their adventures.

"I see," he said dryly. "Someone else has got the dough, eh? Button, button, who's got the button?"

Was it by chance, Peter wondered, that his gaze rested, with just a hint of insolence, on Peter as he asked the question?

Peter realized that he might legitimately be an object of suspicion. He admitted having found a large sum of money, amount unknown, and was the author of a ridiculous story that he had dropped it in a rain-water barrel, slid down a wistaria vine under fire, and left it to its fate. An improbable yarn, to say the least. No wonder Jack Meredith looked at him with that incredulous, supercilious smile. From the point of view of an outsider, what was to have prevented him from hiding the money and inventing this cock-and-bull explanation of its disappearance?

He knew that Janet believed in him, but he wondered whether Carey did not have some doubts. The banker was a hard-headed business man. Practically all he knew of Peter was that he was broke except for his small salary. Twenty-five thousand or so is not to be sneezed at. Many a man's honesty had not stood the test of such a temptation.

Carey did not like Meredith much, at least in the capacity of a future son-in-law. "Who do you think got the money from the bag?" he asked bluntly.

Meredith shrugged his shoulders. "How should I know?

'Who steals my purse steals trash,
'T'was mine, 'tis his, and shall be slave to thousands.'

If I were guessing I'd say someone who knew it was in the barrel."

Peter looked directly at him. "Nobody knew it was in the barrel except me—as far as I know."

"I'm no detective, you know—like you, Mr. Moran. How can I tell who has got the loot? What's your opinion?

For all its casual tone there was something insulting about the way the question was put. Janet bristled up.

"Whatever do you mean, Jack? You don't think any of us have it, do you?" she asked sharply.

"Oh, I didn't imply that. Of course not. I've never known you to rob a bank yet, Janet," he said lightly. "Even if you do take gold bricks from a rain-water barrel."

"I suppose if you had been there everything would have gone lovely," she said.

Peter excused himself. "I'm going back to Petrolia tonight.

113

Want to have another look around Mrs. Farrar's place. I'm not satisfied yet that the money isn't there."

"Call me up on long-distance tomorrow, Peter, will you?" the banker told him.

After he had gone, Janet gave Meredith one long look of cold anger. "Sometimes, Jack Meredith, you can be the most insulting of anybody I ever saw. I believe you think Peter has got that money himself."

"You're a good guesser." He offered her a cigarette and when she refused lit one for himself. "That story of his about the rain-water barrel is just a little bit too fishy. I'm disappointed in him—thought he had more imagination than to spring one like that."

"What makes you think he took the money, Meredith?" asked Carey.

"Everything. Even by his own story nobody else knew about where he put the bag. We're asked to believe that by sheer chance bullets hit the barrel and drained off the water, and then again by sheer chance that somebody came along in the darkness and felt around in the bottom of the barrel to see if anybody had left there a bag full of money—somebody who wasn't looking for the money at all. Of course his story would have been that the thugs came along and got the money, but unfortunately they spoiled that by arriving on the scene to look for it. This didn't leave him a leg to stand on. His fairy-tale collapsed right there. By using our common sense, by the process of elimination, we come back to Moran. Who else could have taken it?"

"You could have taken it—or Dad could have—or I. Any, one of us just as likely as Peter. For instance, take me." Janet's words poured out indignantly, her eyes flashing. "Why don't you accuse me? I found the bag. I was alone with it in the dark car. I substituted the bricks. Why didn't I let Dad and Peter get the money? Because I wanted to steal it. So I hurry up and beat them to it. That's just as plausible as your story."

"Oh, if you want to be absurd," Jack said sullenly. "Of course you'd stick up for this fellow. You always do. But the fact remains that he's the most likely one to have taken it."

"I'd say he was the most unlikely one. It's impossible. That's all. The idea of thinking that of Peter. It's horrid. Isn't it, Dad?"

Her father did not give her quite the unqualified support

she had expected. He took out a cigar, snipped off the end, and lit it.

"Not impossible, Janet. He *may* have done it. We don't know that young man very well. I'd thought of that before Meredith mentioned it. But I don't believe he did. Unless I'm mistaken he's a young fellow of character. I've looked up his record. I like it. Nothing at all shady. But we have to remember that trusted men are always falling by the wayside. Moran may have yielded to temptation and done this."

"I'm ashamed of you, Dad," his daughter cried hotly.

"You needn't be. I'm talking out of a considerable experience of human nature. There wouldn't be any bank defalcations if there weren't trusted employees or trusting employers. But, coming back to Peter—I pin my faith to him as an honest man, in spite of the fact that he may have had plenty of chance to take this money. He has singularly honest eyes."

"Now you're shouting," his daughter told him slangily. "I *know* he didn't do it."

"Oh, of course if you know that ends it," Jack retorted. "Only——"

"Only what?" Janet demanded.

"Nothing. Nothing at all. But I suppose I may have a private opinion of my own, mayn't I?"

"Have all you like," she told him loftily.

"Thank you," he replied with mock humility.

CHAPTER XXIII

Peter is Given a New Room

During the long inter-urban ride back to Petrolia, Peter went over again in his mind the facts in regard to the missing money. He was driven to the opinion that some outsider, someone not connected with the robbery, had found the bag in the water barrel, removed its contents, and substituted the bricks.

Earlier in the day workmen had been busy building the chimney next door. If it had not been for the long, heavy rain he would have thought that perhaps they might have heard the shots, come over to investigate, and made the find. But they were engaged on outdoor work, and it was almost certian that the rain had driven them away hours before. There was a possibility that some chance passer on the street might have done it, but against this theory stood the fact that when he reached the scene the barrel would still have enough water in it to cover the bag.

There remained for consideration the people living in the Farrar house. One after another he checked them off, considering each as a possibility. There was an anaemic school-teacher from New England, absorbed in the routine of her school duties and intent on absorbing culture by way of reading course and summer-school work. It was not likely that she would become involved in a melodramatic adventure like this. Still, it was possible. Then there was the little book-keeper who peered in a near-sighted way at his fellow-guests over gold-rimmed spectacles. Also, not a likely figure for adventure. Both of these lived in the front of the house and neither of them had been, so far as Peter knew, in the house at the time of the trouble between him and the bandits. It had been too early for the book-keeper to get back from work. This consideration probably eliminated Maisie the stenographer, as well as David Summers. But there was more than a chance that Sid Farrar had told David about what had occurred, and that David had done a little private investigating on his own account. Of all those in the house David seemed to Peter the most likely to know what had become of the contents of the brown bag.

This was Saturday night. Tomorrow would find the various members of the household at home more than they were on a week-day. Peter decided to have a talk with as many of them as he could get alone, and in particular with David Summers. There was not much chance that this would lead to anything, but he had to play long shots.

Mrs. Farrar was extremely reluctant to let Peter back to his room. "I want to forget all about this business," she told him. "It's been a dreadful shock to me. I'm still frightened and nervous. I don't say you were to blame, Mr. Moran, but it wouldn't have happened if you hadn't been here. If you would find another place to stay——"

"I will tomorrow, Mrs. Farrar," he promised. "But can't tonight. It's past midnight, and of course all the hotels are full. Besides, if I am here it will be a protection against those men in case they should return."

"I don't feel that way, Mr. Moran. I'd rather not have

116

trouble even if they did come. I can manage them. And I don't expect them to come."

"Neither do I. Come, Mrs. Farrar, I'll not bother you long. Tomorrow I'll get my stuff out. Won't that do?"

She hesitated. Very plainly she did not want him in the house on any terms. He wondered why. The reason she gave was inadequate. There was something at the back of it, some reason which he could not fathom. The very fact that he sensed this made him determined to stay. He knew she dared not turn him on the street the way she had the bandits. To do so would be to prejudice the case of her son when the bandits came to trial. His fate lay largely on the good-will felt toward him by Peter and Carey. If they turned against him he might be held as an accessory before the fact.

"Couldn't you get a room at the Petrolia Arms?" she asked.

"Impossible, with the town crowded like this. I don't see why you are so anxious not to have me here even for a night."

He pushed this home to see what effect it would have, and he was surprised to see what a centre shot it had scored. The words had alarmed her. He saw that at once. She was afraid of arousing his suspicions. It followed then that she had reason to fear.

"Oh, if you make such a point of it you can stay," she said reluctantly. "But I'll have to fix your room up. It's all torn to pieces."

"If I can help you clear up——"

"No, you stay down in the sitting-room. I'll let you know when it's ready."

Left alone in the empty sitting-room, Peter wondered once more just what this meant. She was beyond doubt afraid of him. Why? Did she, after all, have the money from the bag? It began to look like it. And yet—he somehow was assured that she was an honest woman. The quality was intrinsic, permeated her forthright, blunt personality. Had some new development in the case occurred—something unknown to him? If so, what?

It was perhaps fifteen minutes later that Mrs. Farrar rejoined him. "I've put you in the room Hall and Murphy had," she explained. "You'll find it airier and more comfortable, and since you're only to be here one night it doesn't matter. I moved your things."

Once more Peter had a sense of frustrated speculation as to

the cause of this. Naturally she would leave him in his own room and save changing the linen and his belongings. Why had she moved him? Her reason as given to him was insufficient.

In bed between the new clean sheets Peter tried to find an answer to his questions. She did not want him in the house at all. If he had to be there she did not want him in his own room. Why? The door of his room had been open as he passed. Evidently she had nothing to conceal there. Yet the fact remained and he wished he knew the significance of it. He fell asleep before he had found any solution that seemed to him satisfactory.

When he awoke the sun was streaming into the room. Someone was knocking at the door. Sidney's voice called through that if he wanted breakfast he had better be getting up since it had been on the table for a quarter of an hour.

Within twenty minutes Peter had bathed, shaved, dressed, and descended to the dining-room. Several of the other boarders were still at the table. They had with them the Hilltown Sunday papers which were full of the story of the arrest of two of the bank robbers. Evidently the reporters had got at Dunn and Carey and perhaps Janet, for Peter was played up in the accounts given. The two battles with the bandits were described dramatically. So Peter gathered, because when he entered the room Maisie was clamouring to be heard.

"Listen here, folks. My goodness, it musta been an awful fight. Mr. Moran escaped by sliding down the wistaria vine while they were shooting at him. I never did like that Hall. He looked like a low-brow villain, if you ask me. Here's what it says: 'Moran flung himself from the window and——' "

She stopped with a little scream of delight. Her eyes had fallen upon Moran standing in the doorway. "Now we'll hear all about it from the hero himself. Come and sit here, Mr. Moran, and tell us all about it."

"Better let the reporters tell it," Peter said, sliding into the nearest chair. "They have much more vivid imaginations than I have. Good morning, Mrs. Farrar."

Maisie rose from her seat, came round the table, and took the vacant chair beside him. "You're not gonna get out of it that way. This is the most thrilling adventure—just like a movie. Only it really happened, and we're all in it. Believe me, I'm gonna be someone at the office tomorrow. So come across with the story and don't leave out a thrill."

Peter grinned. "There's not much to tell. I cried to him. 'You and I will meet again some day, miscreant.' Then I bounded through the window. He shot me through the heart and——"

"What!" cried Maisie.

"Right through the heart. I staggered back. 'Villain, you have murdered me,' I murmured, and expired almost instantly. The funeral will be at three o'clock Tuesday. No flowers."

"That's not a bit funny," Maisie told him with decided disapproval.

"No, I'm afraid it isn't," he agreed. "But it's the best I could do on the spur of the moment."

"Don't be a crab," the girl teased. "Tell us just how it was, Mr. Moran."

Since there was no escape he gave a very short, dry account of part of the episode. It was so prosaic that Maisie told him when he had finished that she would rather read the newspaper account. "It's heaps more racy. You're holdin' back on me, Mr. Moran. I know you are, and I don't think it's fair. Do you, Mr. Summers?"

It was easy to see that Summers was impressed by what had taken place. He sat on a stool and spent his days with figures. The biggest adventure likely to come his way was a perverse trial balance or the notification that Lafayette No. 2 was spudded in. Like most young fellows he dreamed of something more heroic than estimates of the amount of casing necessary to finish No. 3. Therefore he was full of admiration for the exploits of Peter.

He grinned at him by way of apology for Maisie. She was all right, Maisie was, but her enthusiasm was likely to be embarrassing at times in its exuberance.

"I expect the fellow who does things doesn't like to talk of 'em, Maisie," he said. "When I get two or three ducks, I come back and brag about it, but if I potted lions when they were charging me, I'd probably be shy of talking about it."

The New England school-teacher made an earnest contribution to the conversation. All her contributions were serious and uplifting.

"The lawlessness these days is deplorable. The trouble is the lack of home training and the negligence of religious instruction. If we tried to propagate in the young a proper reverence for the institutions of civilization——"

"Yes, that would be too bad," interrupted Maisie pertly. She had a standing surface feud with Miss Lowell, based on the ground that she did not intend to be "high-browed or high-toned," as she herself expressed it. "How many times *did* this Hall shoot at you, Mr. Moran? And is it true that you won a Croix de Guerre in France?"

Peter was busy with ham and eggs. He wished that Maisie had a little of the "proper reverence" Miss Lowell talked about—at least enough to respect a chap's personal right of reticence.

"I was so busy running away that I'm not sure," he answered. "At the time I was so frightened that it seemed about twenty times, but I suppose two or three times is more correct. And about your other question—I'm sorry, but the French Government overlooked me somehow."

"But the paper says——"

"Yes, these reporters have to make a good story, you know. That's what they're paid for. But I wouldn't take the chaps too seriously." He tried a diversion. "Ever meet any newspaper men? They're happy-go-lucky lot. Always broke. Always good company."

Maisie fell into the trap. "I once had a gentleman friend who was a newspaper man. We had lots of good times. I think he went to China. His name was Bill Arthur. I wonder if you ever met him, Mr. Moran. He came from Chicago, too."

Peter finished his breakfast hastily, asked Summers if he were going to be in his room for a while, and fled before Maisie had gathered her forces for another attack.

CHAPTER XXIV

David Summers Talks

Peter went upstairs to his room. Passing in his light-footed way through the hall, he stopped in front of the door of Sid Farrar's room. A sound had brought him up abruptly—the sound of a teaspoon tinkling on china. Following this came another. He guessed it to be the chink of a cup being replaced on a saucer.

Somebody was in that room eating breakfast. It could not

be Sidney, for he had seen her entering the dining-room from the kitchen as he started to leave. Who then?

The blood drained from his heart as he stood there. Hall, or Murphy, or both of them. Of course. That must be the answer to Mrs. Farrar's reluctance to have him back in the house, the reason why she had moved him so that he would not have the adjoining room to the one occupied by this mysterious guest or pair of guests.

He waited outside for an instant, but there came no other sound. Then, hearing someone coming up the stairs, he passed on to his room. The first thing he did after entering it was to lock the door very quietly; the second to examine his revolver in order to make sure that it was ready for instant action.

The discovery he had made was disconcerting. It disturbed conclusions he had reached as to Mrs. Farrar and her daughter. Was it possible, after all, that these women actually had become involved with Hall and Murphy as accessories? He did not want to think so. He liked them. Unless he was greatly mistaken they were good women, not the sort to have furtive secrets with law-breakers. Perhaps, because of Earl's connection with them, Mrs. Farrar had been coerced to lend them shelter until they could arrange for a get-away. If so, she was not playing fair with him and Carey. But he did not blame her for that if she felt her son's interest was involved. Few women can put abstract right before a personal relationship, and these are not the most lovable of their sex.

But no matter what Mrs. Farrar's reasons might be, they were likely to involve her in trouble. He had done his best to protect her by urging frank co-operation with those on the side of the law. If these men were found now hidden in her house, she would be held as an accessory after the fact. Her son would be treated as a full-fledged member of the gang. She had been incredibly stupid, Peter felt, in not confiding in him.

His mind beat around among the facts in an attempt to find a way out that would not be disastrous for her. He knew without any debate that he intended to turn the situation over to the police. He had not the least intention of precipitating trouble for himself by attempting an arrest on his own either with or without the help of Dunn. It was not his job. He had been quite spectacular enough already, and he could not congratulate himself that he had been particularly successful.

But of course the police would have no consideration for

the Farrars, mother and son. They might even include Sidney in the haul of their drag-net, at least enough to cloud her name and brand her as a suspicious character. It was a hopeless muddle. Peter tried to get comfort from the assurance that it was not his fault, that he had done the best he could for them and they had rejected his help and his advice.

If Hall and Murphy were in Sidney's room, there was at hand a reasonable explanation of the disappearance of the money from the water barrel. They no doubt had recovered it and had it with them in the room.

Peter wondered whether the outlaws knew he was in the house. It was possible that Mrs. Farrar, knowing the bitterness of Hall's feeling toward him, might not have told them he was here. Even though she was forced to hide them she would probably do anything possible to avoid a conflict between them and him. Another battle in her house would be fatal to the establishing of her reputation as an innocent outsider.

It was reasonably certain that the concealed bandits would not appear in the light of day. They would wait till dark before they left the house. Therefore Peter did not feel it necessary to keep an eye on the door of their room.

Having made sure that the passage was free, he very quietly moved down it to the stairway and thence to Summers' room on the first floor. A cheerful "Come in" answered his knock.

Summers was writing a letter, but he pushed pen and paper from him at sight of his guest. "To my mother," he explained. "I write every Sunday. She likes to feel that every Tuesday morning there will be a letter in the mail from me. Take that easy-chair, won't you?"

Peter took the chair, but he swung it round a little, ostensibly on account of the sun but really because he wanted it to face both door and window.

"Maisie was quite determined to have you a hero," Summers said with a grin by way of opening the talk.

"Yes. It's embarrassing, especially when I'm the last man in the world that the word fits. I'm a very quiet chap really, and I don't like fireworks of that kind. The fact is I'm timid. I ran just as quick as I could yesterday."

If Summers was doubtful about his timidity he did not say so. He remembered, however, that Peter had been decorated for bravery and that he had fought the bandits at the hold-up till he had been knocked senseless.

"Afraid you won't be able to persuade Maisie of that," he said.

"People got hold of a darn fool notion about a chap and somehow he can't knock it out of their heads," Peter complained. "I was so scared that I jumped from the window of my room and ran. I should think that would speak for itself."

"It might—if you hadn't come back and captured two of them later," Summers said.

"*I* didn't capture them. My friend Jim Dunn and Mr. Carey did that. I was practically knocked out at the time."

"Well, the papers give you the most of the credit. Say, what do you think became of the other two, Hall and Murphy? According to the papers all the roads were watched. There was no chance for a motor-car to get away. And the trains were kept under observation too. Can they be in town yet, do you think?"

Summers asked the question frankly and ingenuously. This was one of the points Peter had meant to raise, for it was possible that Sidney had told him of the mysterious guest or guests in the house.

Peter looked at the young fellow directly, as though considering. "I wonder," he said.

"I hope they've lit out and we've seen the last of them. Maybe they have. I don't see where they could go in town without being detected."

"No," agreed Peter. "I suppose this is the only house that they know well here."

"Probably." The clerk's answer was matter-of-fact. Apparently it had nothing to conceal.

"And of course they couldn't be hidden in this house anywhere." Peter gave no particular emphasis to his statement. It was merely as though he were eliminating all the factors that need not be considered. But his gaze happened to be full on the face of the other.

Summers shook his head. "No, we know that, anyhow Mrs. Farrar kicked them out. I saw them leaving. Besides you're in their room.

"Of course. Anyhow, a man couldn't be concealed in the house without the other boarders knowing it, could he?" It was a question this time. Naïvely put, phrased in the negative as though it almost answered itself.

123

But in the eyes of David Summers, into which Peter still happened to be looking steadily, came an odd flicker of startled doubt. They asked a question, and that question was, "What do you know?"

So the clerk knew, too, that somebody was being concealed in his sweetheart's room. That made three in the secret, not counting the man or men in hiding. And unless David was a better liar than. Peter thought he was the mysterious guest was neither Hall nor Murphy.

CHAPTER XXV

Peter Locks and Unlocks a Door

From his room, looking through a tiny crack between the door and the casing, Peter kept an eye on the hall. Presently Sidney came up the back stairs, looked up and down the corridor to make sure she was alone, and tapped four times gently on the door of her own bedroom. It was opened. She disappeared inside. Five minutes later she looked out, reassured herself as to the hall being deserted, and slipped down the back stairs with a tray.

Peter waited ten minutes, then moved down the hall and tapped softly four times on the door of Sidney's bedroom. A key turned in the lock and the door opened a few inches.

Simultaneously Peter put his shoulder against a panel and pushed. The unexpected weight did the trick. Peter found himself inside confronting a slim, tall, dark youth. He closed the door and locked it.

"Who the devil are you?" demanded the young man.

"My name is Moran—Peter Moran. Glad to meet you, Mr. Farrar. I've been anxious to have a talk with you."

"Who told you my name was Farrar?"

"Nobody. I guessed it. Your sister has probably mentioned my name. I'm a friend of the family—at least in this matter that has just arisen."

"Oh, are you?" The boy's manner was defensive, wary, even hostile. Peter had expected no less. It was his intention to disarm that suspicion if possible.

Peter had guessed, as soon as he had caught that surprised question in David Summers's eyes, that Earl Farrar had come home. Why he had come Peter did not know. Perhaps his conscience had troubled him lest his mother and sister might fall under suspicion because the bandits had lodged in their house. Whatever had brought him back, he was here. Peter had no least doubt of that.

And this discovery had immensely relieved him. Far better for Mrs. Farrar to shelter him than the outlaws. It is no serious crime for a mother to give refuge to her son, and, after all, Earl had not been a party to the robbery. Probably she had discussed with him the advisability of communicating with Carey, and in all likelihood the young fellow had vetoed the suggestion.

But Peter had decided instantly that he would see the youngster and have a talk with him. He believed he could give assurances Earl would accept, pledges that would come stronger direct from him than second-hand from the boy's mother.

That was why, in modern slang, he had crashed the door.

"I think so," Peter said quietly. "I want to convince you that I am. Shall we sit down and talk it over?"

Earl declined to sit. "I'll stand," he said curtly. In some way he felt he was asserting his independence, his refusal to accept overtures of friendship, by remaining on his feet.

Peter smiled, and his smile, as always, had that something of friendliness which drew men to him. "The way it seems to me it won't do any harm to have a powwow. If we don't hit it off, I can walk out of the house and you'll be no worse off than you are now. And you never can tell; I might have something to say that would interest you."

"All right. Shoot your stuff."

The boy made the concession ungraciously, but he made it. This was all that Peter expected.

"Might as well be comfortable," he said, and he took a chair and found a cigarette. "Have one? No? You won't mind if I smoke, will you?" He rested one foot on a suitcase beside the chiffonier.

"Suit yourself. You make yourself at home, anyhow."

The Sunday paper was scattered over the bed and the floor. Peter took that as his cue. "There's a story in there that interested you as much as it did me, I expect."

"I don't know what you're talking about," the younger man said sulkily.

"I'm talking about the one you're thinking about." Again

Peter grinned cheerfully. "The story about the arrest of your acquaintances Lynch and Tige."

"You claim I know 'em, do you?"

"I don't claim they are friends of yours. I know they are not."

"You're the only honest-to-God real family friend, aren't you?"

"I'll not go that far. Come out of it, boy, and give me a chance. We'll not get anywhere unless you'll lay aside prejudice and size up fairly what I've got to say. Maybe I am straight. Maybe I'm not trying to slip something over on you."

"I'm listenin'," Earl said, still curtly.

"Your sister has probably told you about how I've sized up your connection with these fellows. You trailed with them until you found out what they were up to. Probably they tried to get you to go in with them. You didn't want to do that, so you lit out and left town without letting them know you were going."

"You're quite a wiz on this guess stuff, aren't you?"

"Sometimes I guess right too," Peter admitted. "A fellow can't be always wrong."

"I'm makin' no admissions."

"That's all right. I'll not ask you to make any until you're sure of me. Perhaps I'd better outline where we stand. I'm working for Mr. Carey, president of the First National. I was the guard with the shipment when it was held up. It was a bullet from my gun that killed Spike Slattery. I'm responsible for the arrest of the two men apprehended, and if I hadn't blundered we would have rounded up Hall and Murphy too. I'm against them, and they are against me. All told, they must have shot at me twenty or thirty times. One of their shots put me in the hospital. So there is no love lost between us. They'll get me if they can, and I mean to put them behind bars if I can. They are not only crooks, but murderous ones."

"Yes, I see by the papers you're the white-haired boy that delivers the goods. I guess you don't have to boost your own stock in this state. It seems to be 'way above par. I expect you've got a good press agent. But what I don't get is where I come in. You've just been tellin' me I wasn't in on this robbery. All right. That lets me out, doesn't it?"

"Does it?" repeated Peter. "As you say, I've done some guessing. The police may guess differently. They know you

126

hung around with this bunch of crooks. You were seen with them a lot both here and in Hilltown. You lodged in the house they rented there. From their point of view you were one of the gang. You'd get a shorter sentence because you are younger and because you were not actually present at the robbery. But I doubt whether any jury would acquit you of being an accessory before the fact."

The young fellow moistened his dry lips. The fingers of his right hand gripped the edge of table by which he was standing. "All right. Put it that way if it pleases you. I'm guilty if they are, say. You've got to show me you've hung this on the right fellows. What evidence have you got?"

"Plenty. I recognized two of them. We have the receipt for the house they rented in Hilltown. A lot of the stolen bills have been found on the two men already arrested, and a lot more in the room where Hall and Murphy lived here."

"You've got money found in the room, then?"

In the young man's voice there was a sarcastic derision. Instantly Peter's attention became keyed to find out what this meant. The youngster knew the money had been lost again. How did he know it?

"We did have it," Peter told him. "Another of my blunders. I lost it again."

"Oh, you lost it!"

"Yes, but someone found it luckily."

Farrar's eyes dilated with surprise. "Who found it?"

"You did."

"I?" There was a note of consternation in the boyish voice.

"Yes, after you got home last night and your mother had told the story of what had taken place. You went out in the darkness to have a look round and you found it in the rainwater barrel."

"More guessing, Mr. Sherlock Holmes."

"Yes, but good guessing."

"So you came in here to arrest me, and all this bluff about being our friend is tommy-rot," Earl broke out explosively.

"No, I didn't come in to arrest you, and I'm not going to arrest you. As to being your friend—well, that depends on you. I can't if you won't let me."

"You're trying to fasten the goods on me. Think I'm a fool? Think I've got no sense at all?" The boy's voice was agitated.

"I think you are in a tight place and that you know it and

127

are worried. I think you ought to sit down and figure out whether you can afford to reject an overture of friendship from Mr. Carey through me."

"You come in here claiming I stole some of your money," the boy cried, his voice rising. "Where is it, since you know so much?"

"Don't get excited. What I know isn't going to hurt you if you'll keep your shirt on. In the first place, I don't claim you stole the money. *You saved it for us to return to the bank.* Naturally that gives you a big lift with Mr. Carey and the police."

Earl was, as he had said, no fool. He got the point at once. The hysterical note was absent from his voice when he spoke again.

"If I've got this money where is it?" he asked.

"Well, to take a shot in the dark, I'd say that very likely my foot was resting on it at the present moment."

Peter looked down at the old suitcase. So did Earl. It was not the first time the boy's eyes had travelled to it during the past five minutes. Now he looked up at the other man quickly.

"You know everything, don't you? How did you guess that?"

"You don't keep your eyes trained to stay away from the danger zone," Peter told him with a smile. "So I've been pushing pretty heavily with my foot and find the suitcase doesn't move. There's some weight in it."

"I won't argue it. Maybe it's there; maybe it's not. What are you going to do about it?"

"You mean after I find out for sure that the money is there?"

"I didn't say that." Earl felt the lack of assurance that comes from youth. He did not know what course he ought to follow. He liked Peter's face, his smile, his manner. He admired the way which he had stood up to the robbers at the time of the hold-up and later followed their trail till he had captured two of them. He had just been reading in the paper that Moran had been decorated for bravery in the war. But he did not want to be a trusting fool who would deliver himself to his own undoing. If he let Peter see the money, he would almost be committing himself to a course laid out for him by the older man. They would expect him to turn state's evidence against the robbers. His mother and sister had told

128

him so. This was one thing Earl was resolved never to do. If he had to take his medicine—well, he would have to take it. Under no conditions would he be a traitor to the men who had trusted him. "You've got no right to look in my suitcase," the boy went on. "You can't shove into my room and bully me. I won't stand for it."

"Boy, I'm not bullying you. I'm trying to show you a way out of darned serious trouble. It's not you I'm thinking about —at least not wholly. What about your mother and your sister? The one thing you've got to make sure of is that you clear their names."

"What d'you mean—clear names? Are you tellin' me that they're in this thing?" the boy demanded fiercely.

"Only so far as you've dragged them in by your foolishness. What do you expect? You brought these men here to board. You trailed around with them and became implicated in this job they pulled off. The men came back and boarded with your mother afterward. In trying to protect you she got in bad herself. I don't say she will be arrested. She won't. But there will be a suspicion both against her and against your sister. There's only one way to avoid that. Come clean. Tell all you know. Don't keep back or hide a thing."

"You want me to snitch, to round on the other fellows. I'll not do it." The excited boy brought his clenched fist down on the table. "I may have been a darned fool, but I'm not going to slide out by being a Judas. You can arrest me if you want to. See how far it gets you."

Once more Peter reiterated his promise. "I'm not going to arrest you, but I can't help it if others do. The only way I can save you is by getting you to tell the whole truth. Who are these scoundrels you want to be loyal to? How loyal were they to you? I'm going to tell you."

Four gentle taps sounded upon the door. The two men stood looking at each other for a moment in silence. It was Peter who recovered first. He stepped to the door.

"Who's there?" he asked.

"It's me—Sidney."

Peter turned the key and opened the door. Sidney came in. He locked it again."

CHAPTER XXVI

Earl Decides to Run with the Hounds

Sidney looked from one to the other of them in amazement. She asked, without words, for an explanation.

"I dropped in to see your brother," Peter explained. "We've been having a little talk. He has been suggesting that he run down with me to Hilltown and take the money he found back to Mr. Carey."

It was Earl's turn to look surprised. He had not heard himself make such a suggestion.

"What money?" Sidney asked.

"Oh, didn't you know? I recovered a lot of the money from Hall's room and dropped it in the rain-water barrel when I escaped."

"In the rain-water barrel?" she repeated.

"Yes. Your brother found it there and was holding it to return to the bank. We've been talking it over."

"I'm so glad, Mr. Moran," the girl said eagerly. "I told him if he would talk to you it would be all right."

"There's one point he doesn't quite see as I do," Peter went on. "He seems to feel that he owes loyalty to these men. I'd like him to know some facts about them. I'm glad you happened to drop in. Would you mind answering some questions?"

"Anything you want to ask, Mr. Moran."

"I'd like him, your brother, to realize that they are a thoroughly bad lot and that he owes them nothing. They tried to get him into serious trouble and were ready to leave him in the lurch if necessary. That's true, isn't it, Miss Farrar?"

"Yes, it is. I think that Hall is the worst man alive."

"Does your brother know that you came on them counting the money and what they told you?"

"I haven't had time to tell him much yet."

"Suppose you tell him how they treated you."

"They were horrid."

"What d'you mean? How?" asked Earl.

"They were afraid I'd tell about seeing them with the money, so they scared me. They said you'd helped in the bank

130

robbery and that you were the one who had killed the driver."

"That I killed him?" the boy repeated, astonished.

"Yes, and that if I didn't keep still and they got caught, they'd tell on you and then you'd be—hanged."

"Who said that?" demanded Earl.

"Hall said it mostly, but Murphy said it too."

"Did they frighten you?" Peter asked.

She caught her lower lip with her small white teeth in a moment of agonized remembrance. "I don't see how I stood it," she cried.

"They did more than frighten you, didn't they?" Peter said gently. "Didn't they abuse the power they held over you on account of your fear for your brother to force unwelcome attions upon you?"

"Yes." She looked shyly at Peter. "You know they did. You know how you came in that time and found Hall hurting my arm."

"Hurting your arm! How?" Earl demanded, anger in his eyes.

"He twisted it."

The boy ripped out a sudden furious oath.

"And Mr. Moran heard me cry out, I suppose. Anyhow, he came in and choked him and flung him out of the room. That was why Hall wanted so much to kill him afterwards."

The lad's face was white. "I never liked Hall. Always felt he couldn't be trusted. But Murphy—I thought he was different."

"He was," Sidney agreed. "He bullied me—made me go out with him and—and things like that," she concluded indefinitely. "But I always knew he wouldn't be cruel like that Hall—not in the same pitiless way. There's something—something not human about Hall. Oh, I don't know how to say it. He's bad. Whenever he came slinking up to me, I'd tremble."

Peter looked at Earl and spoke quietly. "These are the men you want to protect, not only at your own expense, but at the risk of leaving your mother and your sister smirched in reputation as having been women associated with a gang of murderous crooks."

"I'll go the limit!" the boy cried. "I'll tell anything you want me to tell. But I don't know very much that's definite. I got in with them, running around with them. Then I felt there was something planned I didn't know about. They would whisper together and break away when I came near. I knew they were cleaning up and getting ready guns. Then one night Murphy told me there was a big job on and that I was to be in it. I didn't want to, and I told him so. He tried to laugh me out of it. When we went back to the others, Hall and Tige looked at each other so queer when I said I didn't want to go in, that I got scared. I had a feeling that they would kill me to keep me from telling. So I pretended to go in and next morning ran away. That's all I know—everything."

"They didn't tell you what the big job was?"

"No. Spike Slattery started to tell, but Hall stopped him. I think he wasn't so very sure about me."

"Probably he wanted to have you help out on it. Then you daren't tell."

"Yes, that would be like Hall," the girl said. "He'd think if he had Earl in his power he could do anything he liked with him. I never knew anyone so—so bad. I hope I never do again."

"What we've been discussing, your brother and I, is the question of running down to Hilltown with this money your brother has found," Peter said. "It's very fortunate that he found it rather than Mr. Carey or I. You see in what a good position it puts us. When he happened to find out about this robbery, he comes back from Kansas City to tell what he suspects, by chance he finds the money I lost, and at once he returns it to the bank. Earl would be sitting pretty. He'd be our star witness, and he would come out of the affair clean as a whistle. I must say that things are working out better even than I had hoped."

"I'm so glad," the girl cried eagerly.

Earl felt himself being driven by an irresistible urge in the direction of law and order. But a certain side of him, the boyish impulse to loyalty, was not yet quite satisfied. He did not want to be an informer, to be smirched with the feeling of having been a betrayer.

"They trusted me," he said lamely, exposing his thoughts and feelings reluctantly, as a boy does. "They figured I'd stand pat or they wouldn't have told me as much as they did I hate to round on 'em. It doesn't somehow seem square."

"How did they trust you?" Peter asked. "They used you for a tool, so that they could lodge at a respectable place like your mother's to avoid suspicion. They tried to take you, a boy hardly nineteen, and involve you in their crimes. They told you nothing, expecting you to trust them without trusting

132

you in turn. They threw you down afterward, threatening to throw the blame of the murder they committed on you who weren't there at all. They bullied your sister by threats to save themselves and to push their unwelcome attentions upon her. They forced your mother to let them go without calling the police, using her fear for you as an instrument, though they knew that if she kept silent she might become in the eyes of the law a party to their crime. You owe them nothing—nothing whatever. But you owe it to your own self-respect to help society rid itself of such vermin by putting them where they can't prey upon honest people."

"I guess that's right," Earl admitted. "Well, when shall we go to Hilltown? The sooner the quicker."

"I'd say by the first inter-urban car that leaves. We'll tell your mother."

Mrs. Farrar was surprised but relieved. She had come to trust Peter, and she knew that the only way her son could save himself was by making a clean breast of all he knew.

CHAPTER XXVII

More Adventures of the Brown Bag

Peter called up Mr. Carey by long-distance and made an appointment to meet him at his house in the early afternoon.

"I have a surprise for you—a welcome one," he said. "I don't want to talk about it over the telephone. If Miss Janet isn't busy, I think she would be interested in it too."

The young men went down on the inter-urban, Earl carrying his old suitcase with him. To look at the battered old bag, nobody would have suspected that it held somewhere between fifteen and twenty-five thousand dollars in it. Yet they took the precaution to deposit it at their feet instead of at the end of the car with the other baggage left there. From the inter-urban station in Hilltown they took a taxi to the Carey residence.

Carey, his wife, and daughter were all awaiting their arrival, Janet at least with ill-concealed impatience.

She came out to the porch to meet them after the two men descended from the taxi. "Oh, Peter, what is it?" she cried. "What have you done now?"

"I haven't done a thing," he told her. "It's this young man who has done it this time. Mr. Farrar, Janet. Miss Carey. And I'd like to know if you're responsible, young lady, for all that blurb in the papers about me this morning. Because if you are——"

"How could we help it, Peter?" she asked, throwing wide her hands. "The reporters just swarmed over us when Mr. Dunn and the officers went in with the prisoners. They talked with him and with Dad, and with me, too, of course. You know how they are. They've got to know everything. But let's hurry in and hear your news."

"Well, I wish between you that you hadn't made me out a regular darn-fool dime-novel hero. I'd like to get off into the hills for a day where there aren't any bandits or reporters or detectives, some place where I could have a beef-steak fry and loaf in the sun."

"Let's do that, Peter," she cried, her eyes shining. "We'll go to Big Rock Park. Let's go tomorrow. No, I can't tomorrow, I'm all dated up. Say, Tuesday."

By this time they were entering the living-room. Peter introduced his companion. The boy sat down shyly, the bag between his knees.

"Glad to meet you, Mr. Farrar," the banker said. "I thought I was about fed-up with surprises, but this is a pleasant one. When did you get in?"

"Last night," Earl said. He did not quite know his status, and he was at an age when embarrassment is easy. Therefore he said no more.

Peter carried on. "Earl doesn't read the papers much and it was several days before he learned of this robbery. He wasn't absolutely sure that it had been pulled off by the men he knew. But after two or three days he became convinced it was and started for home to tell what he knows. I've heard his story, but I want him to tell it to you, too, Mr. Carey, in his own words."

This explanation may not have been literally true, but it was the colour which Peter wanted the facts to wear. Therefore he suggested it, knowing that first impressions endure. Also, he called young Farrar by his first name because it stressed his boyishness.

Carey at once adopted the Christian name, both for its effect upon the boy and for its effect upon the police authorities.

"We'll be very glad to listen to anything you have to say that can throw light on these men and their connection with the robbery, Earl," he said.

The boy did not tell his story fluently. It had to be drawn out of him by questions and examination. There were, as far as he knew, five men in the job—Hall, Murphy, Slattery, Tige, and Lynch. If they had inside help from any bank employee, Earl did not know it. He could see now that they had been planning the hold-up for some time. At that time he was employed, but he had learned from his mother and his sister that the five men met every day while they were at Petrolia for a low-voiced conference. The work on the derrick where Earl was employed gave out. After that he was with these men more. At Hilltown he slept in the house they rented. He had a feeling that some plan was on foot but it was not until the night before he left for Kansas City that any inkling of what it was had been confided to him. He became alarmed for his safety, feeling that he would be under suspicion if he refused to join with them now, and therefore he had run away.

"Why didn't you tell the police?" Carey asked.

"I'd have got a long way, wouldn't I? You can't arrest men on suspicion, or at least you can't do anything to 'em. I didn't even know what place they were planning to rob. They would have been arrested, and in a few days turned loose. Where would I have been then?"

"In very serious danger," Peter agreed. "The police could not have protected him, or at least they would not have done it. I think it was the most natural thing in the world for Earl just to pass out of the picture."

"I think so too, Dad."

"Natural, yes. Still, I suppose it leaves him legally an accessory before the fact. That's merely technical, however. His testimony against these fellows will wholly clear him."

"I should think so," Janet replied with some warmth. Then, her curiosity overcoming her, "What's in that suitcase—some more nice glazed bricks?" she asked.

Peter lifted the suitcase to the same table where the brown bag had been at the time it was opened.

"Shall we let Miss Carey open it?" he asked of Earl.

"Suits me," the young man said.

"This is another of Earl's contributions to the cause," Peter said. He stood back to make way for Janet.

Mrs. Carey came forward too. "My goodness, this is thrilling."

"If it's another of those surprises that carry on to another chapter I'm going to have heart failure," Carey announced with a smile. He did not like to show it too plainly, but his eyes too were gleaming with interest.

Earl handed to Janet a small key. She fitted it to the lock and after she had turned it pushed the catch to the right. Then she raised the top of the suitcase.

Before their eyes lay a pile of silver and of currency flung loosely together.

"No gold bricks this time," Janet cried. "Where did it all come from?"

"Out of the brown bag you rescued from the rain-water barrel," Peter told her.

"Yes, but who on earth got it? Did you?" She turned to Earl.

The young fellow nodded, flushing.

"When?"

"Last night. After I came home. Mother told me about the trouble between Mr. Moran, and Murphy and Hall, and all about the shooting. After I had looked over his room and saw how he went down the wistaria vine—Mr. Moran, I mean—naturally I went down into the back yard to see how he had done it. Then I saw the water running out of the rain barrel where Hall had shot holes in it, and inside the barrel the handles of the bag were sticking up. I carried it to my room, emptied it into my own suitcase. It struck me that Murphy and Hall might come back to look for it, so I took the brown bag back. I thought it would be better if I put something heavy in it. So I got some bricks from the pile a few feet away, dropped them in the bag, and flung it back into the barrel."

"So, that's the last of the adventure of the brown bag?" Janet commented.

"I hope so," her father said. "It's been thrilling enough to suit me without any more chapters added."

"My sentiments too," Peter contributed.

"I've liked it," Janet said, dimpling suddenly.

"I haven't." Peter acknowledged frankly.

"It's been good fun, but of course they haven't been shooting at *me*. That might make a difference."

"Not your fault they haven't," her father said by way of reproof. He turned to young Farrar. "I'm much obliged to you, Earl. You've done a lot for us already. Some fellows would have cached away the money they found and let us whistle for it. And we're going to be able to use you at the trial. Your testimony will complete the case against these men. I think you had better go down with me to the police headquarters and tell your story to the Chief. I want to be sure he gets the right angle on this from the start. He's a little sore because his men didn't pull off the arrests made, and we might as well placate him by seeing him at once and leaving this money with him."

Earl was not at all anxious to meet the Chief, but he did not say so. He had committed himself to a course from which there was now no withdrawal. He did not know that he regretted having done so, but it was clear to him that for better or worse he had to go through with it.

The banker telephoned to the garage and ordered the chauffeur to bring the car.

Janet found occasion to speak a word alone with Peter.

"It's not necessary for you to go too, is it? Mother and I would like to have you stay to tea."

Peter grinned. "I don't suppose it's necessary. Very likely it will be better if I don't go. Probably the Chief isn't waiting for a chance to fall on my neck after the way the papers scored the police this morning and played me up. But I'm not much of a tea hound."

"But you'll stay, won't you, if Mother asks you?"

"Oh, yes, I'll stay. Good of you to ask me."

Janet must have passed the word to her mother, for presently, when the car stopped in front of the house, Mrs. Carey asked Peter if he would not stop and have some tea. Other guests dropped in, and presently Peter found himself talking about the wild flowers of the Rockies with Janet. The two drifted from the living room to the library to verify some point by reference to a book on the subject.

This settled, Janet flung a personal question at him.

"What are your plans, Peter? I mean for your future?"

"I haven't any very definite ones. Perhaps I can get into something at Petrolia. I know a young man—he's a friend of Miss Farrar and boards with her mother—who has some influence with an oil company there. He may be able to get me something."

"I think Dad will have something to offer. I don't know

what. But I heard him say that men like you are rare and he wasn't going to let you get away from him if he could help it. I'm telling you so that when he does speak to you there won't be any inferiority complex in your mind playing down your merits. You ought to learn to toot your own horn a little, Peter."

"What shall I toot it about? I'm not an engineer, or a banker, or a lawyer. I don't quite see how I can be useful to him."

"Don't tell him I told you, and I'm not quite sure, anyhow. But I think it's the Southwest Oil Company. Dad and four or five others are the chief ones in it. There's a vacancy in the place of field superintendent. If Dad gets them to appoint you, don't, for goodness' sake, say you're not an experienced oil man. That's not what they want. They are looking for a man to handle the business end of it in the field. Maybe he isn't what they call a superintendent, but he's a manager of some kind."

"I'll tell them I'm the best man they could find," Peter smiled.

"You are, too," Janet flung up a hand in greeting to a young man lounging through the doorway. " 'Lo, Jack. Guess what's happened?" Then, in swift answer to her own question, "We've found the money taken from the brown bag."

"Oh!" Meredith's comment came after just an instant of deliberate silence. "Did Mr. Moran find it?"

"Not exactly. He found the man who found it."

"I see. That's almost as good, isn't it?"

"And he found the witness we need to convict the men we've arrested."

"Some little finder, isn't he? An oil company ought to get him to locate its well for it. Probably he'd strike a gusher every time." Meredith kept his smile working to rob his sarcasm of some of its sting. "Well, who is the gentleman who found the mazuma and was found by Mr. Moran?"

Janet, inclined to be resentful at Meredith's attitude toward Peter, sensed the hostility behind his words. "I'm not sure I'll tell you any more, Jack. You're so superior."

"Not at all. I'm rather inferior in point of fact. I haven't fought with bandits or arrested them or been in the headlines of the papers. I'm just an ordinary dub."

"Perhaps you're right," Janet agreed sweetly and unexpectedly. "Earl Farrar found the bag. He had come home to tell what he knew about the robbers, or maybe I ought to say what he guessed, and when his mother told him about the fight he snooped around outside and found the bag with the money."

"And then came to Mr. Moran with the news, I suppose?"

"Yes," Janet turned to Peter. "Was that the way of it?"

"Practically."

"Which only proves that the world is full of honest thieves, doesn't it?" Meredith said airily.

"He isn't a thief, this boy," Janet protested indignantly.

"My mistake. I thought he trailed around and lived with them till the time of the hold-up of the express shipment."

"Does it make you a defaulter because you played golf with Milne Jordan?"

Jordan, the defaulting cashier of a local bank, was now doing time in the state penitentiary. Prior to the exposé of his misdirected financial efforts he had been a prominent member of the country club.

"Not the same at all," Meredith said stiffly.

"Quite a parallel case," Janet differed with impish malice. "Earl Farrar played around with some future bank robbers, you played with an actual one. But I don't think you got any of the loot from Milne Jordan any more than this boy Earl got away from his robbers."

"That's very funny, I suppose you think?"

Janet's smile was almost a giggle. "It is rather funny, Jack, come to think of it."

"I don't agree with you. Sorry, but I don't appreciate being compared to an associate of a bunch of murderers and crooks. I dare say my idea of humour differs from yours."

"Don't be so deadly serious, boy," Janet told him. "Come out of it. I'm not doing anything but telling you not to be so snifty about this boy. He's a nice young chap, really. Isn't he, Peter?"

Peter corroborated her appraisal of Earl.

They drifted back to the living-room and had tea, after which Peter took his departure.

Janet went as far as the door of the living-room with him.

"Have you got a date for Tuesday, Peter?"

"To go into the hills?" he asked.

"Yes. To Big Rock Park, say."

139

"I'd like it," he said. "How'll we go?"

"In my car. I'll dig up another pair and we'll picnic. Shall I?" She added as an afterthought, "If it's nice weather."

"Sounds interesting."

"Then call me up tomorrow morning about the details. I'll have our cook put up the eats."

Peter did not quite know why he carried away with him such an absurd feeling of exhilaration. Janet did not mean anything in particular, of course. She was engaged to another man. Still——

CHAPTER XXVIII

An Interruption

By Tuesday the weather had not sufficiently cleared for a picnic into the mountains, but Wednesday was warm and sunny and Janet got Peter on the telephone.

"We're going tomorrow, Peter, if it stays nice. Better take warm clothes, though. You never can tell how the thermometer will behave this month. Come to the house. About ten say."

"I'll be there," he promised. "What shall I bring in the way of food?"

"Nothing. I'm looking out for that."

To his surprise Peter discovered that Jack Meredith was to be a member of the party. It appeared to be equally a surprise to Meredith. Janet's matter-of-course manner assumed there was no reason why she should not have asked them both. The fourth of the picnikers was a gay, bright-eyed young thing with plenty of colour and vitality. She seized upon Peter eagerly and was disrespectfully respectful to him.

"Good gracious, we've got a celebrity with us," she bubbled. "I'm awed. Do you eat a bandit for breakfast every morning, Mr. Moran? Tell me all about it. Tell me whether a hero feels inside just like a plain ordinary everyday——"

"Fresh egg," Janet concluded for her with a grin. "You mustn't mind Elise, Peter. She was born that way and it's never been spanked out of her. When you understand that, and when you come to see that she is a man-grabber and collects their scalps to hang on her belt, then——"

"I do *not*, Mr. Moran. She's probably jealous of me because she can see at a glance you're going to like me and I'm going to like you."

"Thanks awf'ly," Peter told Elise. "Half of that is true. I wish I were as sure of reciprocity on your part. Afraid I'll turn out a disappointment. Usually I do. You see, I don't know anything about young ladies and how to talk with them."

"No, you *don't!*" she derided. "Here's a new line, Janet. I suppose he claims he's shy. It's his way of telling me he intends to sit back and let *me* entertain *him* instead of keeping on his toes."

"I don't know whether I'm shy or just stupid," Peter said.

"*Shy!*" Elise clung to her thesis. She had a way of italicizing words with her voice as she talked. "There's no such animal any more as a shy *man*. They're extinct, like the dodo or whatever it is. Unless it's just your line? Is it, Janet?"

Janet merely smiled. Elise did not need any help in the process of getting introduced to a man.

It was a beautiful day, as winter days are likely to be in the Rockies. The valley through which they drove was bathed in a glow of amber sunshine, and far away the snow-ribbed mountains stood out white and blue in the untempered light, giving an effect of stark, chill nakedness. For a dozen miles and more they rolled along the smooth concrete pavement leading from Hilltown toward the west, then deflected from it to take a good dirt road which led by devious turns on a steady upgrade, to a cañon which cut into the foothills as though it had been hacked out of them sheer by titanic sword-cuts.

There was some snow in the hills, though it had been, as a whole, a dry winter. The drifts lay blanketed above the road among the pines, and when the car reached the summit of the foothill range, the mountains of the continental range still looked far and drear.

They were in Meredith's car, and he was in the driver's seat with Janet beside him. Peter held a little grudge at Janet. She ought not to have let him in for a picnic with Jack Meredith, and especially in his car. She might have known that Peter did not care to be under obligations to a man who did not take the pains to hide his unfriendliness. He suspected that she did know, and that she had deliberately brought the men together in the hope that a better understanding would dissolve the antagonism between them.

They crossed a wooded park and took another road which wound along the shoulder of a hill, dipped into a draw, and from it climbed to the lip of a park which nestled high among the crags. It was a saucer-shaped basin, and on one slope was a cluster of great rocks, which gave the place its name. This outcropping of quartz covered two or three hundred acres, and below it was the small stream which wound its way from a lake at the foot of an immense snow-capped peak. A glacier fed the lake.

Just above the big rocks Meredith stopped the car. Its occupants descended, taking with them rugs, baskets of food, thermos bottles, kindling to start a fire, and a gridiron upon which to cook steak.

Janet took command. "Jack, do you want to start a fire? And we're going to need water. There's a spring over there, Peter, behind that flatiron rock, the one with the red streaks on the face. You can help me, Elise, if you want to be useful as well as ornamental, and I know you do. We'll find a place for lunch and get things out."

Peter took the canvas bucket and followed the trail which led down to the spring among the rocks. The water trickled rather slowly and it took some minutes for the bucket to fill. While he waited he lit and smoked a cigarette. He thought of Janet. These days, unless his mind was consciously focused upon something else, it was likely to slip into meditation about her. She was so animate with life, so keen, her smile so warm with friendliness, that it was natural he should like her. So he explained to himself his interest in her.

He picked up the bucket and started back along the trail. He heard voices, though he could not make out the words. Yet it struck him that one of the voices was harsh and strident, and this rather surprised him. Meredith spoke usually in low, soft tones. He and Janet had both been in good spirits and very companionable on the way from town. Anyhow, he was sure this was not Meredith's voice. He was not disturbed, but he moved a little more rapidly.

Then, abruptly, words rang out crisp and menacing. "Don't move, any of you, for ten minutes. Stick right where you're at. Get me? There's a guy in the rocks will bump you off if you take a step."

Peter dropped the bucket and began to run. As he did his

142

right hand was dragging at the gun in his coat. The weapon was a bulky one and Peter had thought about leaving it at home, but the past few days had made him cautious. There was a chance, one in a million he had reflected, that he might meet Murphy or Hall. Therefore he had it in his overcoat pocket.

There came the sound of a starter, of the purr of a motor. The path rose rapidly toward the bench above. Another dozen yards brought his eyes on a level with the surface of the plateau. He saw Janet, Elise, and Meredith standing in a row, their hands raised above their heads. The car was swinging around in a circle to take the road. Who was driving it he could not see, but he knew it was a hold-up of some kind. For target Peter had the choice of a rear tire or the gas tank. He chose the latter because it was larger.

His first shot came instantly as the weapon fell to the level. His second was fired so quickly that the two sounded almost as one. The car plunged across the brow of the hill. It vanished a second later.

Peter ran along the path to the ledge they had selected for a camping ground. The revolver was still in his hand.

At sight of him Elise gave a scream and flung her arms around the neck of Meredith, who turned so as to screen her body with his own.

"It's Peter!" Janet cried.

Her hands went out to his impulsively, instinctively. "We've been robbed!" she cried. "And they've taken the car."

"They'll not take it far," Peter answered.

CHAPTER XXIX

Janet Recognizes an Old Schoolfellow

After Peter had departed to get the water, Janet began to sort the baskets, setting out food, paper plates, cups, knives and forks, and linen. Meredith built with flat rocks a three-walled fireplace, arranged paper and the kindling, then with a hatchet in his hand moved away to get some wood. He strolled in the direction of the pines. There would be dead branches full of resin which would roar to a red heat in spite of the recent rains.

He had perhaps gone forty of fifty yards when a sharp cry brought him up short. He turned, to see Elise crouched against a rock wall and Janet standing rigid, while two men with automatics confronted them. Meredith did not hesitate an instant. As quickly as possible he ran back to the camp site which he had just left, at the same time calling out that he was coming.

One of the men, the smaller of the two, whirled to meet him. The gun covered the young man as he approached.

"That'll be near enough for youse," the man behind the gun snarled.

Meredith stopped. It was the only thing he could do, unless he wanted to commit suicide by forcing the other to fire.

"What's it all about?" he demanded. "Why draw a gun on these ladies?"

"Say, young fellow, we're asking the questions an' giving the orders. Don't youse forget that. An' move over there by the skirts, with your hands up. See?"

Jack Meredith took his place as directed.

"You don't need to point your guns at these ladies. They are not dangerous. What is it you want of us?"

"Where's the other man, the guy that was with you?" asked the larger of the two hold-ups.

"He went to get some water."

"All right. We don't need him. Fling that grub back into the baskets, and all the rest of your contraptions. Those thermos bottles too. No, the skirts can do that. You keep yore hands right up in the air. Haven't got a gun, have you?"

"No," Meredith told him.

The smaller of the two men—he was an evil-looking, pasty-faced fellow with cold and cruel eyes—helped the women put the food back into the baskets.

"It just happens we haven't had any grub for two days, or none to write home about," the big man explained roughly. "So we'll have to take what you've got and borrow the car. Got plenty of gas?"

"About ten gallons, I should think. Maybe not so much."

"That'll do. Drift along back to the car—all of you."

Elise began to sob.

"Stop it," barked the smaller man. "Pull hysterics here an I'll slam you over the head. Get that straight."

Meredith lowered an arm to slip it under the elbow of the frightened girl. His fingers closed on hers.

144

"It's all right, Elise. Don't be afraid," he comforted.

They moved toward the car in a little procession, the two outlaws bringing up the rear.

Janet was white to the lips. She knew these men would not hurt her or Elise or even Meredith, unless he lost his head and showed fight. But if Peter's name should be mentioned, if he should return before they had gone, she was quite sure that they would murder him. For after the first shocked moment she had been certain that these two men were the two missing bank robbers. Evidently they had been driven to the hills because their escape had been cut off. They dared not stay in Petrolia another hour longer; the roads had been blocked and the railroads watched. No doubt they had discovered that. In the darkness they had probably slipped down to the river, followed its banks to the thick willows, and cut across the mountains to hide in some of the caves in Big Rock Park. At least that was Janet's guess.

What she knew for sure was that if they learned that Peter was the fourth member of the picnic party they would not leave until they had killed him. Her heart ached with dread lest they should not get off before his return.

The supplies were put in the car. Hall took the driver's seat. Murphy glared at the three before him. "Stick your hands up and keep 'em up." Then, after he had been obeyed, he gave them orders not to move for ten minutes or another man would shoot them from the rocks.

In another moment he was in the car beside his confederate. The motor began to sound. The driver swung the car round in a half-circle.

There came the crack of a gun—a second. Elise screamed. The robbers had said there was another man watching them from the big rocks and she supposed he was firing at them. Then a man plunged into sight over the brow of the hill and her arms went around the neck of Meredith for protection.

The man was Peter. He carried a gun in his hand. There was a faint thin trickle of smoke hanging about the end of the barrel.

Janet flew to meet him, crying out the news of what had happened. They had been robbed of their luncheon. The men had taken the car.

When Peter said that they would not take it far, she asked why not.

"I hit the gasolene tank twice, low down. They'll run out of gas," he explained.

"That's bully, if you're sure," Meredith said. "They can't get out of the hills unless they make the raise of another car. We'd better broadcast the news, so as to head them off."

"Where's the nearest telephone?" Peter asked.

"The park superintendent lives across at the other end of the ridge. I suppose it's half a mile—or perhaps three-quarters. Probably he has a 'phone."

It was surprising what a change had come over the attitude of Jack Meredith toward Peter. He no longer felt any sense of insolent exasperation. The reason he did not know, but it lay in his psychological reaction to the situation. He had rehabilitated his reputation before Janet and Elise. He had not done anything extraordinary—nothing that any man would not have done. But he had taken a fighting chance of being shot when he returned to support the girls, and he had shown the two scoundrels that even when they had him covered with a gun he was not afraid of them. Jack felt quite friendly to the world at large, including Peter.

"One of us ought to go over there and get a call through to police headquarters at Hilltown and another to the Chief at Petrolia. As you say, we'll have these fellows bottled up in the cañon if we move fast enough." This was Peter's suggestion.

"Good enough. Shall we all walk across?"

"Don't you think I'd better stay here to stop any car that might come up from the Corona road? Otherwise it might go on down the Hilltown road and be commandeered by these fellows."

"You're talking sense," Jack agreed. "All right, I'll move over and take charge of the telephoning."

"I'm going with you," Elise announced promptly.

"You'd better both go with him," Peter said.

"Why had we?" Janet asked. "I don't see any need of it. I'm going to stay here with you."

"I believe I'd go," Peter advised. He did not care to explain to her a possibility that had occurred to his mind, that when the car stopped for lack of gas, as it would very soon, the bandits might choose to return to Big Rock Park because it offered such good hiding facilities. His theory was that they would try to slip back unnoticed, would lie concealed till night, and would then cut across the mountains to some point where they could jump a freight train.

She smiled at him, in the manner of a friendly enemy. "I believe I wouldn't. Why should I?"

"Well, I just thought——"

Peter stuck. If he explained what was really in his mind, she would be more than ever obstinate about staying.

"It doesn't matter much whether she stays or goes, Moran," the other young man said. "If she wants to stay, why not let her?"

Peter shrugged his shoulders, metaphorically speaking. Probably his reasoning had been rather far-fetched anyhow. If she insisted on staying, why not.

So it was decided.

"It may be some time before I can get the line through to the points I want. When I do I'll come back. If you pick up any news of any kind—say, if some car passes them in the canon—Janet can bring word to me so that I can fire it on down to those below," Jack said.

After the others had gone, Janet walked with Peter to the edge of the plateau from which they could look down into the crater where the big rocks were massed.

"I suppose they've been hiding here several days," she said. Then, abruptly, her eyes swinging back to his, "You know, of course, that the men were the two bank robbers—the ones you call Hall and Murphy. I haven't seen Tim Murphy since I was a little girl, but I knew him at once."

"Did he know you?"

"Don't think so."

"I guessed that was who they were. I'm glad to know for sure," Peter said.

"Why didn't you want me to stay with you?"

"I didn't see any need of it."

"Why not tell the truth, Peter? You were afraid they would come back. You think now they will. You didn't want me with you if they came for fear of trouble. That's why you wanted to send me away."

Peter was surprised at the correctness of her guess. "Why should I think they'll come back?" he asked.

"Because their one hope was to get through the canon before the road was stopped. If the car runs out of gasoline, they are balked. But they have food with them to last a day or two. Probably they'll come back and hide in the park and cut across the mountains during the night. That's what you thought."

"Is it what you think, Miss Mind-Reader?" he asked her with a smile.

"Depends how far they get in the car. If they discover the tank is leaking and plug up the holes with cloth, they may get down through the cañon. If they get even five or six miles they won't walk back. At least I shouldn't think so. They will work out of the cañon directly into the hills."

"Sounds reasonable. But I don't think they'll get that far. There must be four bullet holes in the tank, all of them rather low. You see, I was firing from below the ledge. The gas will shoot out in streams. It would be hard to plug them even if they try."

"Are you sure you hit both times?"

"Quite sure. I could hardly have missed. The car was close to me, and I've had a lot of practice at targets both during and since the war."

"Then that's that." She questioned him, the lovely brown eyes in the eager face quick with life. "What do you mean to do Peter? Are you going to try to arrest them?"

"No. Not my business. I'm through interfering with police jobs. But I thought I'd hide and watch them if they come back. Then when the officers come, we'd have a line on where they are."

She thrilled. "Oh, Peter, I'm glad I stayed with you. I hope they come back."

"Different here," Peter said bluntly. "I hope they don't."

"Don't you want them caught?"

"Yes, but I'd like to quit subbing for the police. I've had a lot of luck up to date, but my luck won't stand forever. One of these days, if I don't let these fellows alone, I'm liable to be a very dead amateur detective. I wouldn't like that."

"I wouldn't like it either, Peter. But if we stay hidden they won't see us."

"If we stay hidden too closely, we won't be able to keep tabs on where they go. So we'll compromise if they come back. You'll stay hidden, and I'll trail them." He announced this quite definitely.

"Peter," she told him, "I believe that if you were married you'd bully your wife."

"Much more likely she'd bully me."

"What kind of girl would you marry? I can't somehow see you married, Peter."

"How do I know? A fellow never does know until his time

comes. No use writing out specifications when you're not going to stick to them."

"Oh, but there is," she differed. "One has to have some kind of plan to work from. What would she be like, Peter, as far as you can tell? Little, I've a notion, and a flaxen-haired blonde, and rather helpless probably. Like David Copperfield's Dora."

"You've quite an imagination," he said dryly.

"And pleasantly plump. Be sure she isn't the kind that runs to fat when she gets a little older, Peter."

"She isn't going to be that kind of girl at all." It was a part of Peter's heritage of lack of confidence in himself that he always had to assume a boldness not native to him. Now he looked at Janet and studied her coolly. "Since we're predicting, I'll offer my guess. The one I'm picturing is not at all like the one you've described."

"So you have thought of one. How thrilling, Peter! Is she a real girl, or just an imaginary one?"

"Not any of your business," he came back with a grin.

"I knew that before you told me. Well, Peter, paint your picture." She slanted a smiling, curious glance at him.

"She'll be rather tall and slender, but not any reed, mind you. Plenty of flesh and bone to give her strength and stamina. A bit of an athlete, I think, but not the kind that shows it in angles and leanness. Eyes brown and long-lashed. Rather wonderful eyes, sometimes kind and frank, and sometimes bubbling with laughter, and once in a while stormy; but always very expressive and quick to life."

"Dear me, this is going to be a poem," she murmured, to the scenery as it were.

"Red hair—masses of it. Glorious red hair."

"She'll have a temper, Peter," the young woman warned.

"Well, yes. I rather think so. But she'll probably control it. I'll teach her to do that."

"Oh! Then you *are* going to be a bully."

"Not necessarily. She'll be so fond of me that she'll discipline herself, especially when I'm around."

"And he claims to be a shy, modest man," she said, once more to the scenery.

Of course he was only answering her raillery. He didn't mean it. He couldn't mean it, Janet told herself. None the less, the blood in her veins quickened with excitement. He had described her as the girl he was going to marry. It rather took her breath away, even though it was just foolery. There was an excess of colour in her cheeks as she changed the subject.

"Wouldn't it be a good idea to look around among the big rocks and see if we can't find where they've been staying?" she suggested.

"I think it would," Peter agreed.

CHAPTER XXX

Janet Makes Deductions

"We might walk along the path to the spring," Peter suggested. "They must have gone there since the rain to get water. There ought to be tracks left by their boots. If so, perhaps we can see in what direction they point."

"Let's," she agreed.

Peter followed her along the path. He noticed how lightly she carried her straight slenderness, how she seemed to move without effort as though it were her will and not her muscles that carried her.

The trail under their feet was a gravelly one, made of disintegrated rocks that had slid down through the centuries from the ledge above. Peter pointed out to her that there would be no footprints unless it was close to the spring, where the seep of the overflow had made the ground spongy.

"I'll not go too near," she said. "Not near enough to tramp them out if there are any."

But there were none even there.

Her companion's trained eyes took in the lie of the land. There was no other trail from the spring. If they got water here they must have come by the obvious path. But it was possible that there might be a point along the path where they had left it to get down to their hiding-place.

Peter suggested this, and as they went back his eyes watched the lower edge of it to see if there was a break where boots had torn down the dirt or the shale. Janet, too, was watching eagerly, keen to be in the heart of this adventure of man-hunting. There was a thrill in it, a big thrill, and it might become a much more intense one if the hunted should double back on their tracks.

They came to the break. There were marks where heels

had slithered down the shale slope and left slight scores. Peter, moving in front of Janet, made no comment. He wanted to give her the chance of discovering these herself. She did.

"Oh, look, Peter, look!" she cried. "Someone left the trail here. See?"

"You'll do," he told her, "I was wondering whether you would see that. Let's see if you can follow down from here."

Janet figured the problem out aloud. "It would be in the big rocks, the place where they stayed, both because they would want to be hidden and because they would want shelter from the rain. They'd choose the easiest way to climb up for their water, so I'd better zigzag to the left where it's not so steep and rugged. Am I right, Peter?"

"You're right if I'm right. Let's keep our eyes open for any marks made by shoes. We may find little scars where heels have dug in on the way down."

"Here's one," Janet cried presently. "Or is it?"

They stooped together, heads close, over the marking.

"I think it is," Peter agreed. "See where the heel first began to gouge its way down, pushing down with it a little dirt and loose rubble, which is banked here at the place where the heel stopped sliding."

"They probably stayed in these first flatiron rocks just below us," she ventured.

"A good guess, and probably a true one. We'll see if you're right."

She glowed with excitement. "Isn't it fun to be able to work so much out from so little? I never thought of it before, but I suppose those scientists—geologists and anthropologists, you know—who reconstruct the early life of the world feel that way when they begin to build up a theory of extinct life from little data gathered here and there and fitted together."

"Probably science is a lot of fun to the sharks who follow it up," Peter agreed. "Here we are. Their camp ought to be among this group of rocks unless we're barking up the wrong tree."

Peter's hand rested on the revolver in his coat pocket. It was hardly possible that the bandits could have got back yet, even on the assumption that they would come at all. But he did not intend to let himself be surprised if he could help it. They might have had a companion with them, still hidden in the rocks, though it was unlikely.

151

As they circled in and out of the rocks, passing between the big slabs, Peter was again in the lead. He had suggested that it was better not to talk out loud and advertise their presence, adding that of course he had no reason to expect that anybody was here.

Janet's hand fell on his arm. "Look, Peter;" she pointed to the black ashes and charred wood of a dead fire.

"Was it *their* fire, do you think?" he asked her in a low voice after he had picked up some of the charcoal and let it sift through his fingers to the ground.

She got the point at once. "Must have been," she whispered eagerly. "The coals are dry, but they would still be soggy from the rain if the fire hadn't been burning since it stopped raining."

"Go to the head of the class," he told her with a smile. "Now you stop here for a minute while I go on alone. There would be a little cave under that slanting slab of rock, and they may have gouged it deeper to sleep there where it was dry."

He drew his gun and moved forward, noiselessly, to look around the edge of the first projection. He presently passed beyond it out of sight.

The young woman's heart began to beat faster. She waited tensely, all her senses keyed for the sound of the possible shot that might shatter the stillness.

None came. She crept forward a step or two. A footfall sounded. Around the corner came Peter.

"No, they've gone," he told her. "But that's where they camped all right. It must have been cold comfort during the rain the night before last, if they were here then, and I think they were."

"They'd have a fire, I suppose."

"Yes, after darkness fell. The fire is just out from the rock. Of course that would help." He turned to another phase of the situation. "We'd better be getting back to a place where we can keep an outlook for them. They probably won't come by the road. They'll leave it and come up through the undergrowth in the valley. Very likely they won't return to their old camping ground at all."

"Is it time for them to be coming, do you think?"

"Probably not yet, but we can't tell. They may have discovered at once the holes in the gasolene tank, tried to plug them, and given it up right away, leaving the car in the road."

They moved across the red ground, coloured from the decomposed sandstone of which it was made, to another group of huge out-cropping spars. The central one projected skyward like a church steeple. In fact, the group was known locally as "The Church." To the foot of this they walked and began working their way up it, or rather up the strata from which the spire ascended. It was an easy climb. There were hand- and toe-holds conveniently placed, and after a few moments of observation Peter knew that this lithe, slender girl was as surefooted as himself.

"This will do, I think," he told her presently. "We've got to be sure they don't see us. That's more important than it is to see them."

They had come to an irregular slanting surface that corresponded roughly to the roof of the church of which the jutting spar was the steeple. In this there were depressions where they could lie with little danger of being seen as long as they were prone.

"Too bad we haven't binoculars with us," Janet said regretfully. "We could pick up moving objects in the valley so much easier with them."

"Yes," assented Peter. "And while we're wishing, I wish they had left some of the lunch they walked off with. I'm hungry as a bear."

"Me too," agreed Janet ungrammatically, but with emphasis. "And it was such a good lunch. I looked after it myself. Fried chicken and olives and devilled eggs and cake and hot coffee——"

"That'll do. You've said enough already to ruin my day."

For half an hour they lay there. The warm sunshine baked the rock pleasantly, so that its heat passed into their bodies and made them comfortable. Occasionally they turned in order to relax flesh and muscles against which the hard rock pressed.

"There's someone down there in the valley," Peter said suddenly. "See! Look just to the left of the big pine that stands alone. Wait. He's hidden now behind some brush. He's coming out now. There are two of them."

"Where?" Janet called. "Yes, yes, I see them now. They're moving this way. I believe they're coming up into the rocks. They are. See! They've turned to the right into that grove of aspens."

"They may stay there and not come up any farther.

They're in a hole and probably don't quite know what to do. The way it has turned out, they made a mistake holding us up for the car, because now they have been located and the search for them will concentrate on this part of the country. Perhaps they won't wait till night to try to cross the range. That's the trouble. We can't see from here. They can slip out from the lower end of the aspen grove into that gulch and get out of the valley unobserved. If they do that before dark, of course they'll run the risk of being seen and reported. But—we've got to know, Janet, whether they go or stay. I'm going to slip down to find out."

"Oh, Peter, I wouldn't. If they see you——"

"No. I've got to go. If we know they're here, the police can surround the grove and drive them to surrender. But they would lose a lot of time if they don't know that they are there. They'll have to be stalked, you see. They can't be rushed without loss of life."

"Then, Peter——"

He stopped her, looking as stern as he could. "Now, look here, Janet. I know exactly what you're going to say. Well, you can't go. That's all there is to it. I've been reasonable. You have to admit that. I've let you stick around here with me when I shouldn't have. But there's a limit, and we've reached it right now. You go over to the superintendent's place and wait for me."

"Let's wait and see if they come up out of the aspens," she suggested, hoping that circumstances might arise which would make it unnecessary to fight out the issue.

They waited. Peter hoped that they would appear on their way to the rocks. But he did not expect to see them. After a time he spoke.

"Sorry, but Mohammed isn't coming to the mountain. I've got to drift down."

He crept down the roof of the slope until he could rise without danger of being seen. Janet followed him.

She rose and faced him. "Peter," she said, "I don't want you to go." He noticed that her lip was trembling, that her eyes were troubled.

"I don't want to go any more than you want to have me," he said. "But I can't sit here, carrying a big gun, and let them slip away because I haven't the nerve to trail them. I'm not going to try to arrest them, and I'm not going to let them see

154

me if I can help it. All I want to do is to find out what they're up to."

"Yes, I know that, but you always get into trouble with them. I know perfectly well they'll see you. Peter, when I ask you not to go, when you know I'll be wretched all the time you're away——"

Peter felt the throbbing of his heart beneath the coats. He told himself it was absurd. Naturally, since she felt friendly, she did not want him to be shot. It was ridiculous to suppose, because she was dear and sweet to him, that her interest betokened any special feeling. None the less he tasted the thrill of exultant joy.

"Don't worry about me. I'll be all right—dear." He gulped the last word out, almost in spite of himself.

"Yes, but you know I shall. I can't help it. Peter, let's go to the park superintendent's house. He'll be there—and maybe some of the workmen—and Jack. Probably they'll have guns. You can go down together."

Peter gave that a moment's reflection. "No, we wouldn't get started for an hour or more. I'll go down and scout, then come back with what information I gather. You go to the house. Tell them what we found out and what I am doing. Have Meredith gather together what men and arms he can. I'll be back, say in an hour—or maybe two. We'll have something definite to go on then."

"Please, Peter," she begged.

He clamped his jaw. He would have liked to be persuaded, but he knew that if he gave way to her he would despise himself later. If he had been a casual outsider there would have been no obligation upon him to go down into that clump of aspen. But he was not. He had volunteered on this man-hunt. He could not quit just because he did not like the position of the hunted. His situation was that of a lion-hunter who has wounded one of the jungle kings and driven it into the shelter of dense undergrowth. There had been no obligation on the hunter to wound the beast, but having done so he could not with self-respect walk away and give up the hunt. So it was with Peter. He must see the job through, though he did not at all like to do it.

"I've got to go," he said. "Don't you see I have?"

His straight look at her demanded an honest answer. She put her feelings outside the case and thought for a moment.

His point of view was sporting. She knew that if he saw it that way, since he was Peter, he had to go through.

"Yes," she admitted. "I see you have."

"Thanks. See you later," he said, as he turned away.

"The best of luck," she called after him.

Peter smiled, a little doubtfully.

CHAPTER XXXI

Big Game in Cover

Since Peter was going lion-hunting he did not neglect the obvious precautions. He preferred to flush his game rather than be flushed by it. It might make more difference than he cared to consider if he should be seen by the outlaws before he saw them. The trouble was that this was not, strictly speaking, a fair fight and no favour. Peter was bound, as an officer of the law, not to shoot on sight. He could fire only in actual self-defence. But no such restriction bound Hall and Murphy. They would drop him without a moment's hesitation.

Therefore Peter did not descend briskly from the big rocks into the valley. He made a wide circuit with intent to reach the aspens from the cañon end of the grove. Below the rocks, to the right, stretched a long slope covered with scrub oak. In the fall, after the early frosts, the foliage of this burned the hillside with a glorious blaze of red, from flame to mahogany shades. Even now many of the dead leaves clung to the branches, offering shelter to one creeping through carefully in such a way as to take advantage of the cover.

Below the rocks, unfortunately, there was an open stretch of fifty or seventy-five yards—a boulder field where to a certain extent he must be exposed to observation. There was a reasonable chance, he felt, that he might get through this without being seen, since there was a gully where he would be partially hidden.

At the limit of the big rock area Peter hesitated before making the plunge forward into the smaller boulder field. If there was any other way—but there was none. He crouched low and moved into the more open territory. Fortunately he was wearing a brown overcoat which tended to blend into the surrounding landscape.

He did not run across the boulder field. Instead, he moved rather slowly, trying not to catch any casual eye which might sweep across the landscape. It seemed of course an interminable time before he reached the gully, yet it could not have been more than twenty-five yards from the point of big rocks where he emerged. He felt the most conspicuous object on the landscape. If the outlaws were in the aspen grove, they would of course be watching the bluff above for signs of activity, in which case there was little likelihood their eyes would miss his moving figure. He hoped they did not have a rifle with them, for if they had one he would be a pretty mark. This did not trouble him much. In the first place, he did not think it likely they had a rifle; in the second, at that distance they could not recognize him without powerful field glasses. Moreover, they were not looking for trouble, but for a chance to make an inconspicuous exit.

Once in the gully, he crouched low and moved down it. The depression was less than an arroyo—was merely a channel where water was carried down after heavy rains. But it was better than nothing in that it afforded cover where bushes fringed its edge.

Presently the gully swung farther to the right and widened into a draw which descended into a small cañon. This, Peter judged, was the one which led to the lower end of the aspen grove. He was getting closer to his quarry now; that is, if they had not left long ago on their tramp across the mountains with a railroad line as the objective.

Peter looked at his watch and was surprised to discover that he had been more than an hour making the descent to the gorge. Very carefully, scanning every bush, rock, and hollow before him, he moved toward the entrance of the gulch. He came to a bend which brought him within sight of the aspens. Crouched behind a boulder, he lay watching the grove for a few minutes for signs of life within it.

He observed none. By following close to the stream he could get such protection as was afforded by the brush growing along the borders. He decided to try to get closer.

Scrambling down the bank, Peter moved forward, every nerve taut, every sense alert. Sometimes he was in the stream itself, sometimes on the moss or the rocks which were rooted close to it. He did not take a single step without first satisfying himself as well as he could that nobody was waiting to ambush him. Very slowly, at such a tortoise pace that another half-hour had passed before he had covered the hundred yards between him and the gateway of the cañon, he crept to the cottonwoods which rose as a barrier to the aspen grove.

Kneeling behind one of these trees, it occurred to him that he was once more in the position of the lion-hunter who has come close to his game and dare not press the issue. If he had been actually hunting lions he could have peppered the grove with a twenty-two in the reasonable expectation of finding out whether his majesty was actually there, or he could have thrown stones as jungle beaters do in the hope of hearing the lion roar.

And with that thought in his mind there flashed to Peter's brain a perfectly logical and feasible plan of procedure.

He shouted in a clear voice, "Look out, you fellows, that they don't get out of the grove and beat it for the big rocks."

Instantly he heard the sound of crashing branches in the young aspens. The two bandits, startled by this shout, which told them they were almost surrounded, were waking to action.

Weapon in hand, Peter's eyes were fastened upon the grove. He could not be sure that the men were not making for the cañon instead of for the big rocks. Logically, of course, if they accepted as true the information he had shouted, they would either stay in the cover of the jungle or they would make a long dash up the hill for the rocks in the hope that they could lie hidden there till nightfall. But he did not know that they would act logically. Under stress of emergency their brains might function in unexpected action.

For some moments the sound of crashing among the young trees continued. Then it died away. Either they had reached the other side of the grove and were scudding up the hill, or else they had decided to lie hidden in the aspens on the chance of standing off an attack till night.

Peter wished he knew which option they had elected. For he had to work his way through the grove to get in touch with them. He could not afford the time to go back up the cañon, follow the draw, and make a wide circuit as he had done in coming down.

He was reasonably sure of one thing: the sound of the crashing through the bushes had grown fainter before it died away. Therefore the men had been moving from him rather than toward him. They would not be at this end of the grove. He left the cottonwoods and ran toward the aspens. Reaching them, he wormed into the thicket with as little noise as possible. Once within its shelter, he crouched low to take stock of his surroundings.

The trunks of the young trees were not thicker than his wrist. They rose tall and straight, a dense growth of them. But there was no underbrush. He could see a distance of fifteen or twenty feet in front of him. Since this was the case he was in no danger of stumbling on Hall or Murphy a foot or two away. He could move fairly rapidly, though care had to be taken against making enough noise to warn of his approach.

He crept forward, revolver in hand. It was a chancy business. If they were in the thicket the chances were that they would see him first, since he was moving and necessarily snapping twigs and stirring the tops of the young trees. Peter did not like to think of that. But he had to keep going.

Never before had he noticed how noisy are inanimate things. The branches and tree trunks seemed to be in a conspiracy against him. They snapped and groaned and rustled at the least touch. More than once the breaking of a dead limb sounded like the crack of a pistol. He wished he had not let himself in for this. The hidden men, if they were here, could not help hearing him as he came.

A shot rang out. The lowest branch of a sapling fluttered down upon him. It had been cut off sheer by a bullet.

Simultaneously there came a crashing of agitated branches, the thrashing of something heavy through the young trees. Peter knew the outlaws were in flight. He rose and charged after them.

The branches whipped his face and hands. His foot caught and he was flung headlong. He rose, his cheek bleeding, his coat torn. Once more he plunged in the direction of the diminishing rustle.

The thicket narrowed. Peter swung to the left and presently emerged from it. His glance swept the slope above. Two men were breasting it on a run, headed for the great rocks.

Peter did not follow them directly. He continued to angle to the left, reached the growth of scrub oak, and pushed rapidly through it. He was in no danger now and he could go at whatever speed he chose.

Making a wide circle to miss any chance of coming upon the hidden bandits, Peter worked up the slope until he reached the rock rim of the plateau. He found a place where the rock fall was broken and climbed to the level above. A hundred yards from him was the house of the park superintendent.

Peter made for it at once. He heard voices and as he came to the gate saw three men near the back of the house. One of them was Meredith. The front door was flung open and Elise appeared.

"Oh, Mr. Moran, we've been so frightened for you since Janet came back and told us. Is everything all right? Did you find them? And did you see Janet?" she cried.

"See Janet? Where?" asked Peter.

Meredith and the other men had come forward at sight of Peter.

"Isn't she in the house there with you?" Meredith wanted to know.

"No. She went out just a little while ago. I thought she was going to join you, Jack. Then I saw her walking along the road—that way." Elise pointed in the general direction of the place where Meredith had stopped the car a few hours earlier.

Peter's heart seemed to turn over within him. He knew where she had gone—to "The Church," the rocks up which she had climbed with him. She had gone in the hope that from that point she could look down and see him coming back. The suspense of waiting had been too much for her. From her point of view it would be a perfectly reasonable thing to do, one without any danger at all. She did not know, of course, that Peter had just driven the bandits back up to the Big Rocks.

"She's gone to look for me," Peter said to Meredith, and he wondered if he looked as white as he felt. "To a place where we climbed this morning, in the Big Rocks, a place they call 'The Church.' "

"Janet's a fresh egg," Meredith said irritably. "She's got no business to go wandering off alone. I suppose there's no danger, but——"

"There wouldn't be—if I hadn't just driven Hall and Murphy up from the valley back into the Big Rocks," Peter interrupted.

"Good Lord, maybe they'll see her coming," Meredith groaned. "We'd better get a move on us."

"So much the better, if they see her coming," the park superintendent said. "They'll keep hidden. They're not looking for her. It won't get them anything to advertise where they are by letting Miss Carey know."

Peter nodded. "But if she meets them by chance?"

They were already hurrying along the road.

"That wouldn't be so good," the superintendent admitted.

"What would they do to her?" Meredith asked.

None of them answered. None of them knew. But Peter could guess what Hall would do if she stood in the way of his escape. He would not hesitate to destroy her any more than he would hesitate to shoot a rabbit.

Peter's pace quickened to a run.

CHAPTER XXXII

Don't You Know Who I Am?

Janet watched Peter go with a sinking heart. She wanted to cry out to him that she had changed her mind, that she could not let him go. But she did not do that. She clamped her teeth and watched him vanish. Then, swiftly, she went back to the road and walked along it to the house of the park superintendent.

The door was opened by a plump, motherly woman, who admitted her when she gave her name. She heard Meredith's voice at the telephone, but he hung up as she entered the dining-room. Elise was just sitting down to a luncheon of fried eggs and bacon with hot cakes and syrup on the side.

She jumped up to meet her friend. "Just in time, Janet. Mrs. Davidson is saving our lives. This is Mrs. Davidson. If I'd had to wait a single minute longer for the eats, I'd 'a' passed out sure. Where's our friend the hero? Is he still watching at the post of duty, like the burning deck boy, whence all but him had fled, you know?"

"We've seen the men that robbed us. They've come back," Janet said.

"Come back!" Elise and Jack said together.

"Yes. I suppose their gasolene all ran out soon. They're down in the valley below the Big Rocks."

"What are they doing there?" Jack asked.

"They're hiding. They want to get over the range and strike the railroad probably. We don't know whether they will lie hidden till night or whether they have started already. Peter went to find out."

"How do you mean to find out? Is he going to ask them whether they are going to stay?" There was a touch of sarcasm in Meredith's voice.

"No. They're in a clump of aspen. He's going in to see if they are there." Janet's voice broke a little. "I begged him not to go, but he would."

"What do you mean that they're there and then in the next breath he's going to see if they're there?"

"I mean that we saw them go in, Jack, but there's a gulch runs from the bottom of the draw where the aspens are. Maybe they are following that gulch into the hills. Peter says we have to know if they are still in the aspens so that the police won't waste any time there when they come."

"Well, I think it's darn foolishness, if you ask me."

Janet delivered her message. "He said he'd be back in an hour or so, and for you to gather what weapons and men you can. If they are down in the aspens, it will take a good many men to drive them out."

"Why would they still be in the aspens?" Meredith wanted to know. "Naturally they will be hot-footing it across the hills."

"They must know the police are wiring and 'phoning everywhere to look out for them. They don't know they've been seen coming back, so Peter says they may lie doggo till night.

The park superintendent had come into the room. "Something in that. Nobody would ever look for them down there. I've dug up another gun, Mr. Meredith. It's an old army Colt."

"Peter says for you, please, to wait till he gets back before you do anything."

"All right. Nothing much we can do, except keep a man on the road above the Big Rocks watching. You'd better sit down and have some lunch, Janet." Meredith held a chair for her and she slipped in wearily. "Don't you worry, old dear," he told her. "Your friend has the Indian sign on those birds. He'll turn up in an hour or two fresh as new paint the way he always does. I've got to give it to him. He's a go-getter. Very likely he'll come dragging them back with him. Never can tell with him what he'll do."

Janet discovered that in spite of her anxiety she had a very good appetite. During lunch she learned from Elise and Meredith what they had been doing. Evidently the telephone had been pretty busy, for they had talked with Hilltown, Petrolia, and several other towns. The officers at these points were watching the roads and it was not likely the outlaws could get away.

"I've talked with Mr. Carey," Jack told her, as he helped himself to some more hot cakes, "and he says for me not to let you get into mischief."

"Oh, I'm all right. I'm worried about Peter." Janet had to stop a moment to steady herself before she went on. "I—I wish he hadn't gone. He said he was going only to try to find out about them. But if they should see him——"

"How do you know these men you saw were the same ones that held us up?" asked Jack.

"We don't—for sure. But Peter was expecting them to come back when the gas gave out. So when they came, and went into the aspen copse, we felt practically certain."

"Sho! Might have been a couple of boys hunting rabbits. Much more likely," Jack dogmatized. "I don't agree with him. Not at all. They're trying for a get-away. They're not coming back to the place where they know there's a fellow with a gun ready to shoot at them, a fellow who has already taken a couple of cracks at them. He's right about one thing, though. They're not going to get very far in my car. Elise and I noticed as we came along the road that there were two or three trails left by the gas shooting out."

"They may have come back," the park superintendent said, after consideration. "What else could they do? They were shut in by rock walls. Chances are they hiked down to the creek and followed it back up to the park, just as Mr. Moran figured they would. Naturally they would come in down in the valley and not up here on the road where they would be more likely to be seen. I guess he's got the right fellows spotted."

"Is there anything to be done now, Mr. Davidson?" Janet asked.

"I guess we've done about all we can except to put a man on the road to keep a lookout. I'll attend to that now. Of course you young ladies don't need to worry about those fellows coming to the house here. They're not going to do that, not after they know we've been warned that they're in the vicinity."

"I'm not worried about that," Janet said. "I wish they would come. Then we'd know where they are."

163

"Gee, I don't!" Elise shivered. "I don't ever want to see a gun again. Honest, Mrs. Davidson, if I ever have another man point a gun at me I'll pass right out of the picture. I never did like Bill Hart's stuff, anyway. It's kinda *crude,* don't you think? And when the director gets his scenes gummed up and lets the villains walk off with the two *beau-u-tiful* heroines' picnic lunch—well, all I got to say is that the scenario hasn't the continuity that gets across to little Elise and has too much suspense. I like thrills all right, all right, *but——*"

After lunch Jack went out with Mr. Davidson into the yard. Janet presently followed them, to see what they were doing. She was too nervous to stay long, and she returned to the house. Elise was curled up in a big chair writing the story of her adventures to a particular friend in the Harvard Law School. She was more or less engaged to him, and he was about fifty per cent engaged to her. It was a convenient arrangement, one which did not interfere with more immediate love affairs in case any such developed, as from time to time they did. Janet wandered around the room, tried to look at a motion-picture magazine, attempted to compose herself before the fire, and abruptly put on her coat again to go out.

"What makes you so restless, Jan?" her friend asked. "I never saw you with the fidgets before. I'm usually the one that can't light."

"I can't stand it, Elise—this waiting. I don't know what's happening. It gets me, just to sit here while maybe they are killing him."

Elise took in with a swift look her friend's troubled face, a look which held both keen scrutiny and alert curiosity. She had never seen Janet so much worried before. Her mind searched for a reason, and found one at once—the reason that would have occurred to any young woman—that had, in point of fact, more than once come to her already.

"You used to know Peter in school, didn't you?" she asked.

"Yes, a little. Not very much. He was shy, I think. . . . I don't see what's keeping him" She looked at her watch. "He's been gone quite a bit over two hours. You don't think, Elise——"

"No, I don't. Peter Moran can look after himself. Besides" —with characteristic audacity Elise fired a centre shot—"he's got to be at the wedding, so there can't anything happen to him."

Janet stopped buttoning her coat. "Whatever are you talking about?"

"It wouldn't be legal without him, would it? The groom has to be there, you know."

They were alone, Mrs. Davidson having retired to the kitchen.

"You trying to be funny, Elise?" demanded Janet.

"No, dearest." Elise giggled. "But it is rather funny, come to think of it, being engaged to one man and in love with another. I should think you'd get quite a kick out of it."

"With your imagination you ought to write books," said Janet severely as she walked out of the room.

She decided to go and take just one little look or two down into the valley. It might be she would see Peter coming. With this in mind she walked along the road toward that point of the Big Rocks where she and Peter had stood together.

It was ridiculous what Elise had said. Just like her, of course. She could not think of any man except in terms of love. Of course, Janet admitted to herself, she did like and admire Peter very much—more than any other man she knew, in some ways. But just because she was anxious about him it did not follow that she was in love with him. How could she be when she was engaged to Jack Meredith and of course was in love with him? A girl couldn't be in love with two men, could she? So that settled that.

"I wish he would come back," she said to herself for the hundredth time. "It's not fair to go off like this and leave me to worry. I'm going to tell him so too."

A man was running along the road toward her. It was the one sent out by Davidson to keep a lookout.

Janet stopped him. "Has anything happened?" she asked.

"Yep, lady! The boss told me to hurry back to him if anything did. There was a shot, down there in the aspens."

Her heart turned over. "Just one."

"Just one. An' then two birds come runnin' out You better look out." He shouted it back over his shoulder, for he was already making time down the road.

Janet hurried on, trying to keep down the tumultuous agitation that seemed to stifle her being. One shot in the aspens, and afterwards two men running out. What of the third man? Where was he? Her leaping imagination flung out terrible pictures—pictures of a man lying in agony, desperately wounded, his weight bending back the slender trunks of the young trees; of a body sprawled face down, hands outstretched, all the supple life stricken from it, muscles lax and loose.

She must go to him—now—as quickly as she could. No time to turn back and tell the others where she was going. He might need her. At this very moment she seemed to hear his weak voice calling her name.

And the quickest way to reach him was through the Big Rocks. Just here she could not get down on account of the rim rock, but a little farther along she would find a place where it shaled off and left an easier descent.

She found it, crossed the path to the spring, and reached the first of the great red rock slabs which jutted from the earth. In and out among the rocks she weaved, moving lightly and quickly as she began the descent, lowering her weight from boulder to boulder or from slithery rubble to loose shale with sureness of foot.

She wished she had remembered to tell the man where she was going, so that Jack could bring help down for Peter. It had been stupid of her, she reflected, but she could not turn back now to remedy the oversight. There was an imperative urge in her to get to him as soon as possible.

At times, when the terrain made it possible, she broke into a little run. She must hurry—hurry—hurry.

She was now in the heart of the big rock area, completely surrounded by them as she dodged to and fro among them or clambered over outcroppings and lowered herself by finding hand and footholds in crevices.

From one of these rock faces she reached a ledge which for a moment looked like an *impasse*. But a narrow path, which sloped sharply, led around a great jutting spar of red stone. She followed this, found herself once more on less precipitous ground, and moved around the base of a second rock mass.

Abruptly she stopped. Her heart missed a beat. She stood face to face with two men. But the one she saw, the one upon whose evil face her fascinated eyes fell and were held by the glittering menace of his, was the man Skate Hall. He stood there crouched, teeth bare, grinning horribly at her, an automatic in the hand which rested upon his hip.

She gave a gasp, and without her own volition moved back a step or two until she brought up with her back to the wall.

Hall followed, keeping pace with her retreat, his eyes for once not sidling but direct, holding hers as a rattlesnake does those of a bird under the spell of impending death.

"So here we are again, miss. Glad to meet up with you, since I can't bump into the guy that queered our get-away. Mighty nice of you to come down an' pay us a visit," he jeered.

"I—I didn't know——" she faltered.

"You didn't know we were here? Now don't spoil it," he mocked. "An' us so set up because you dropped in for a friendly call."

"I thought——"

"But now you're here you'll stay, won't you? You'll not go rushing off, ma'am? Don't do that."

"What about him?" she asked. "Did you—did you shoot him?"

"Meanin' one of the guys down in the valley? I sure hope we did."

He used an oath that shocked her by the intensity of the malice with which he bit it out.

"Don't you know?" she asked.

"Say, what's eatin' you?" he snarled. "Who is this guy you're so anxious about? What's it to you whether we did nor didn't?"

He came closer.

His face, his eyes, his manner were indescribably menacing. Janet thought for a moment he was going to shoot her where she stood.

The other man came forward. "Why did you come down here, miss?" he asked roughly.

Janet took her eyes from the pasty, snarling face of his companion.

This second man had a heavy, lowering countenance. He looked a ruffian, but not like a devil from hell.

Under swift impulse Janet said what was in her mind.

"Don't you know me?"

"Sure I know you. You were in that car we took."

"Yes, but—don't you know who I am?" Then, swiftly, "I went to school with you."

Tim Murphy looked hard at her. "I give it up," he said at last. "What's the answer?"

"I'm Janet Carey. Don't you remember? In the eighth grade at the old Lincoln School."

"You're—Sorreltop," he said.

"Yes."

She took off her soft felt hat. The sun's beams glinted in her glorious red hair.

"Say, what is this pullin' on me—a Sunday school class reunion?" demanded Hall. His suspicious glance shifted from the young woman to Murphy and back again. "This stuff don't get anywhere with me. Not none. I don't fall for any shenanigan. See?"

Murphy glared at him, and Janet knew instantly that the two men hated each other, that only the extremity of their common peril held them together.

"None of your business," the big man growled. "Don't try to bluff me. If this young lady and I want to talk—why, we're gonna talk. Get me? An' you'll keep your mouth shut."

They had spent nights in the rain, without food, without shelter. Their nerves were worn ragged, their tempers ready to flare at any trifle. In the mind of each had arisen a grievance at the other, one that needed only a spark to explode like powder.

For a moment they stood facing each other, crouched, snarling, like wild animals at bay, each holding his automatic close to the body, ready for instant action. Janet leaned against the rock wall, not breathing, paralyzed by fear.

It was not till afterward that it came to her how close to herself the danger lay, that if Hall killed Murphy he would never leave her alive a witness of the crime.

Then, sullenly and reluctantly, Hall made his decision. He chose not to fight, not here, when the odds were even and there was no room for treachery.

"Say, what's the big idea in crabbin' at me, Tim? This blest-be-the-tie-that-binds stuff don't make any hit with me. I tell you that straight. But if that's your line, why go to it."

The fellow's voice was half a whine, half a threat.

"I'm playin' my hand the way it suits me," Murphy told him, his voice harsh and bullying. "I'll not stand for any interference. See? I'll settle what's to be done about Miss Carey. Me, Tim Murphy. Bite on that hard, you yellow cur."

"All right! All right! Keep your shirt on. I've already said— ain't I?—that I'd stand for anything in reason? What more do you want?"

Janet breathed again. For a brief moment at least the

shadow of red tragedy had lifted. She appealed to Murphy in a low voice.

"Let me go. I'll not tell anyone I saw you. But I must get down into the aspen grove. I must—I must."

"Why must you?" demanded Murphy.

"To help the man you shot before it is too late."

"What man? Who is he?" the big man asked.

The name "Peter Moran" was on her lips, but in time she stopped herself. "He's the man who—who has charge of the park," she said.

"What's he to you?"

"A friend. I know him. Please let me go. If he is hurt and I can help him——"

"You'll stay right here," Murphy told her roughly. "I don't know as he's hurt, anyhow. If he is, serves him right."

She pleaded with him, for the sake of their old school days, but the big bandit trod down her appeal, almost savagely.

"It'll be dark in another hour," he conceded at last. "You can go then, if you've a mind to, after we've struck the cañon. But you're not leaving here till we do. No use squawking about it either."

Janet leaned against the rock wall and wept. She had a conviction that Peter had been hurt. Her heart ached to go to him, but she knew quite well that she would have to stay here until Murphy gave the word.

CHAPTER XXXIII

Two Shots

Peter made straight for the point of rocks which he and Janet had climbed a few hours earlier. He expected to find her there, far up on the sloping rock which formed the roof of what was known as "The Church." He was consumed with a fever of anxiety to reach her, to get her as soon as possible out of the danger zone.

His first thought was of her. But associated with this was the knowledge that Hall and Murphy too were in the Big Rocks section, that at any moment he might by chance come face to face with them. Therefore he carried his revolver in his hand, ready for business instantly.

He dropped down from the road on the plateau into the rocks, crossed the path to the spring, and hurried toward the point for which he was heading. The spire pointing skyward rose above the other freakish outcroppings and made the place easy to find.

Presently he found himself at the base of the masses of rock up which they had climbed. He called to her, at first in a low voice, then louder. His shouts brought back only the echoes of his own voice.

No other answer reached him.

Peter hesitated. Should he ascend to the roof in search of her? But why? If she were there she would answer. He could not afford to lose time. In less than an hour now it would be dark. If she was lost, or if she was in the hands of the outlaws, night would bring to her additional terrors and perils. He must make the most of such daylight as remained.

Sick at heart, he turned away. Instinctively he knew that she was somewhere among the Big Rocks—unless indeed she had passed through them on her way to the aspen grove.

But no—she would not do that.

Not even Janet would be so foolhardy, since she had no way of knowing that Hall and Murphy were not still lying hidden there.

What could he do, except wander around in the red rocks looking for her? That was no pleasant outlook. It would be just as likely that he would find the two hunted outlaws instead, in which case, if they heard him coming, he would get short shrift.

The early dusk of winter in the Rockies began to fall. Objects at a distance grew less distinct. The far mountains took on the purple tint of coming night.

Occasionally Peter stopped to call out, not too loud, "Janet! Janet!" He did not want to betray her presence to the outlaws in case they had not seen her; nor did he want to handicap her, in case they had found her, with the stigma of being a friend of those who hunted them.

Peter's heart jumped. From below where he stood, not far away, there lifted the sound of a voice. He listened, keyed to high tension, every faculty alert. There were two voices.

The words he could not make out, but it was plain that men were arguing.

Quietly he moved forward, in and out among the rocks, descending with every step. A great flat rock angled out of the earth and barred his way. He climbed up to the top to look over the edge, for he knew that those disputing were just below.

"She'll go back an' tell 'em, don't you see? They'll have us inside of an hour. No chance for a get-away if——"

The voice was whining and ingratiating. The one that answered was savage and gruff.

"Nothin' doing, you yellow cur. I'll not have the girl hurt, I tell you. They get us or they don't get us. We'll play for the breaks, but whether we get 'em or don't—you'll—not—touch —a—hair—of—her—head. Get that straight."

"All right. All right. But I'm tellin' you, Tim, how it'll be. She snitches an'——"

Peter reached the edge of the rock and looked down. They were there, just below him, the two men and the girl. Hall lifted the palms of his hands in reluctant surrender, half-turned away, and at the same instant his right hand dropped as though by chance to his coat pocket.

Suddenly he whirled, automatic in hand, his face distorted by passion and hatred.

A shot rang out—two of them.

Hall stood, dazed, his face a map of puzzled wonder fading into agony. His knees sagged. The automatic fell clattering from his fingers an instant before he pitched forward on his face.

"My God!" Murphy cried. "How—who——" Peter spoke. "Don't move, Tim. I've got you covered. Listen. I beat him to it. That's the answer."

Crouching against the face of the rock, Janet came to life.

"Peter!" she cried. "I thought—I was afraid——" Then, with a break in her voice, "Is he dead? Have you—killed him?"

"Yes."

"He had it coming," Murphy said bitterly. "The coward tried to gun me when I wasn't looking."

"Exactly that," agreed Peter. Another thought was in his mind, one he did not put into words. This was that the villain would have murdered Janet as soon as her protector was out of the way.

"If it hadn't been for you, 'Fraid Cat——"

Peter for once did not correct the appellation, but Murphy himself did.

"I mean Peter," he explained.

"Let me do the talking, Tim," Peter said quietly. "The cañon down there is open. There wasn't anyone down there with me when I drove you out of the aspens."

"That was you, was it?"

"They'll be down here from above in five minutes now they have heard the shots. You'd better try the cañon. It's your best bet."

"You mean—I'm free to go?"

"Yes."

"What's the idea?" growled the man below, suspicion in his voice.

"The idea is that you saved Miss Carey's life. Far as I'm concerned you can hit the trail. But the law won't look at it that way. You'd better go now."

Ungraciously, because he did not know how to speak any other way, Murphy growled, "Much obliged." He moved forward to where the other bandit lay, stooped down, and turned over the body.

"You got him right," he said, rose, and vanished around the corner of the rock.

It took Peter only a few seconds to get down to the ledge where Janet was.

Instantly, by no volition of their own apparently, she was in his arms, clinging to him, sobbing, crying out broken words to relieve her pent emotions.

Peter held her there, tightly, soothing her with words of love and gentle caresses.

"I thought—I was afraid—— Oh, Peter, if they had killed you!"

She shuddered, and he felt the beat of her heart against his body.

He knew she had been in far greater danger than he, but he did not tell her so. Some day, when the shock of it was gone, they would talk over all that each had suffered in fearing for the other.

But not now.

Gradually she regained control of her emotions. Peter drew her away from the ledge where lay the crumpled body of the bandit and climbed with her to another level place above.

The reaction from their fears brought another mood—one of warm elation. Peter felt surging in him the glow of victory.

He loved her. She loved him. Nothing else in the world mattered. .

He told her so.

She gave him her hands and her lips.

Presently she asked him shyly a little smile in her eyes, "Are you thinking of asking me to marry you, Peter?"

"I did think of it," he admitted quietly, answering her smile.

"Don't!" she said. "Not till tonight. There's something I've got to say to Jack first."

"That you can't marry him owing to a subsequent engagement?" he guessed.

"That's it. I haven't treated Jack very well, Peter. You see, he was right and I was wrong. I've been too interested in you ever since you came back. But I didn't know it then. Still, it can't be helped, can it? And Jack won't really mind very much. He's begun to see that it wouldn't do for him and me to get married. I think he'll really be relieved after the first shock."

"Let's hope so."

They walked in the gathering darkness toward that future which lay before them radiant and alluring, and as they went forward their fingers found each the other's and laced themselves together. It was to be that way with them always now, each thought.

Renegade by Ramsay Thorne